Attempting Flight

Attempting Flight

a collection of short stories

by Raven Wolfe

Cover art & book design by Raven Wolfe
and Bo von Hohenlohe Productions.

ISBN-13: 978-0692870006
ISBN-10: 0692870008
Library of Congress Control Number: 2017904973

Raven Wolfe Studio
Goleta, CA 93117
www.RavenWolfeStudio.com

Dedication

I dedicate this book to Lilian and George Meiselman. My parents lived their dramatic lives right before my eyes and they taught me the complexity of family entanglements, insatiable passion, humor and great love. My father told me I could never be a writer because my handwriting was illegible. But then he bought me a typewriter. Once I learned to type, it changed my life.

Thanks Dad.

Acknowledgments

I would like to thank all those who encouraged me to believe in myself as a writer. To my beloved teachers, Joan Fallert, Patty Cohan, Janet Lucy, your kind support and encouragement continually brings me back to my greatest passion–writing. To all the members of writing groups, classes and workshops, you reassured me that what I have to say is important and worthy.

To the late Ginny Cashman and my PRH group, you embrace my words and inspire me to write from the deepest parts of myself. Each of you, in your own way, has fortified me to listen to my inner voice. To trust what comes forth from my wild imagination and, most of all, to honor myself as a writer. Utmost gratitude to those of you who allow me the privilege of sharing my stories with you.

And specifically to my support team who pulled me through the rigors of self-doubt. To Kate Dillon, Cary Keogh, Grace and John Ferry, DJ Zayha (Dr. John), Brian Silsbury, Karen Hartfield. You have each, in your own way, sustained me with great love and conviction. To Karen Greenberg, a true artist, your encouragement and assistance has pulled me along. To Erik O'Dowd, who has loved each and every story I have sent his way. And to Bo von Hohenlohe, who has guided me and worked with me to design a finished product I can be proud of. If you had enough hair to pull, I am sure you would have pulled some out in the process; bless you for making me laugh. Dore Gardner, you nudged me with such patience and tenacity that I was forced to surrender my resistance. To Paul Zakrzewski and Chris Alderman, thanks so much for your attention to detail. And I especially want to give thanks to all my friends who sat quietly and listened (or pretended to) while I read my stories out loud. You never snored, even when you fell asleep. I would especially like to thank my characters, who tell me their stories and show me the way into their minds and motives, their secret desires.

And to Heather, Aryn and Geoffrey, you continually remind me that I am a work in progress. I love you more fiercely than you can imagine. You, more than anyone, inhabit my most tender heart.

"We each receive the world according to our lights
and what the sparking loop of our senses affords us
and all I can do is hope to capture it in an individual way, to
represent the phenomena that crowd in on us
through every conscious moment
as they appear and vanish again."

T.C. Boyle

Contents

Boating with George

"OK. Next weekend we're going boating." This announcement, a huge surprise to all of us, comes at the dinner table. My father, between mouthfuls of brisket, explains that he's going to borrow a boat from one of his friends and then we'll all go to Turkey Foot Lake on Saturday. I imagine a little rowboat with an outboard motor.

"George, do you know anything about boats? Because I don't, so you'd better know what the hell you're doing."

"How hard could it be?" he asks in a feeble attempt to reassure my mother, who shakes her head. She knows something.

At Turkey Foot Lake we wait in line, watching the other boaters stealthily back their boat trailers down the cement ramp into the water. Eventually the boat would rise up off the hitch and someone who had been sitting in the boat disconnects it, starts the engine and drives the boat over to the dock to wait for the rest of their party to park the car, run over to the dock and get in the boat. Smooth as silk. My father watches, smoking and saying "Uh huh. OK. I see how it's done."

Once it's our turn, my father does everything he's seen the other boaters do. The first problem—backing the boat straight into the water. He has to start over about 23 times. A crowd gathers. He waves to the crowd good-naturedly. My mother stands in the boat, waving her arms, trying to direct my father to back the boat straight.

1

"Need help?" a man wearing a hat full of fishing hooks asks.

"Nah, I can do it. Thanks, anyway."

"You done this before?"

"No, not really, but I can figure it out OK." The line behind us gets longer and people start honking their horns. No one can proceed until we get our boat into the water.

"OK Lil. I have an idea. You go stand behind the boat and guide it into the water once I've backed the trailer to the edge of the lake." My mother looks at him suspiciously. She stubs out her cigarette. My brother and I are in the back seat pinching each other. As far as I'm concerned, the day is shot. I'm sweating like a pig and my hair has already frizzed itself into a helmet the size of a small suitcase.

Very slowly my father, his face slick with perspiration, backs the car down the ramp, frantically watching his rear view mirror, checking out the side view mirrors. The crowd makes encouraging sounds and eventually I can see through the back window that the boat is floating in the water.

"It's floating" my brother and I yell in unison. My father jumps out of the car, running to the edge of the lake.

"Lil! Lil!" he calls frantically. "Oh my God, Lil. Where the hell are you?" The fear in his voice propels my brother and me out of the car. We run to the end of the ramp, where the boat bobs peacefully in the water, no sign of my mother. My brother starts giggling. He points. My mother's head is emerging out of the water, her sun hat still on her head, her hair hanging in her face.

"You goddamn son of a bitch. Next time you stand at the end of the boat." The crowd cheers and claps. My father looks embarrassed, but mostly he looks relieved.

Once my father starts the outboard motor (which takes several tries), we putt putt across the lake. The boat, a small cabin cruiser, is way too large for our simple needs – a drive around the lake and some lunch that my mother had packed. My father announces The Plan—to find a shady spot near shore, drop the anchor and eat cold chicken, my mother's famous potato salad, some cookies and Cokes and sweet juicy peaches. And probably some chips. And maybe some peanuts. Perhaps a peanut butter sandwich. Maybe even a bunch of grapes. (My parents don't believe in skimping on food.)

After about ten minutes of driving across Turkey Foot Lake, the motor fails and my father is unable to restart it. He's humiliated. He's pissed off. He makes derogatory comments about the friend who lent us the boat. Then he swears for about ten minutes. It's hot on the water. The lake sends up a blinding glare. We decide to eat lunch on the boat while my father continues to struggle with the motor.

Other boaters pass us and offer assistance. My father, of course, insists he can figure it out on his own. My mother has resorted to smoking and drinking vodka and orange juice out of a thermos. My brother and I take our paper plates of food down into the cabin, but it's even hotter down there. Besides, there are spiders. We resort to teasing each other until my mother threatens to come down.

Once my father has drunk all the beer and has resigned himself to never being able to start the motor on his own, he acquiesces and accepts one of the many offerings to start the engine. Afraid to turn off the motor, we head back to the boat launch, where my father, already defeated, allows someone to help us get the boat back on the trailer.

"Well. That was fun, wasn't it? Didn't we have a great day?" He laughs about the part where my mother went under the water at the back of the boat. He raves about the chicken and the peaches and the beautiful day. His enthusiasm inoculates us all with pure joy. It was a great day. We laughed, we ate, we got wet. Who could ask for more?

"You know, the next time we'll borrow the speed boat. I think it'll be easier to handle." My mother glares at him out of the corner of her eye.

"Over my dead body."

She was Killed by Cabbages

She was killed by cabbages. It's something that will always be said about her in almost mythic tones and those knowing looks that convey a vague sense of irony. At some point, that was all that set her apart from any other woman of her kind. It will be forgotten that she was 35 years old at the time of her death, that she had a pack of Marlboro's in the pocket of her red western shirt, that she had a name and that she lived her life in the realm of extremes. All that will be remembered is that she was killed by cabbages, actually crushed under a ton of cabbages—crispy green with tough beautifully furled outer leaves.

Her name, Soledad, described her in totality. Alone. That is how she lived, after the brief period of her childhood, which ended when her mother committed suicide. Her father, who was generally referred to by her mother as "the sperm donor," hadn't stuck around long enough to see her tiny brown body slide out of its dark cave three months earlier than she should have. Her mother described her early arrival as her daughter's attempt to see "the sperm donor" before his untimely departure. This is the story she told to neighbors, cousins, shop keepers and anyone else who would listen as she wheeled Soledad through the neighborhood in an old umbrella stroller.

"Yeah, she thought the jerk would be here when she popped out, but he had already left. The bastard. Left me with this one in the oven, just kickin' her way tryin' to get out fast enough to see him." She was named Soledad by an aunt who thought the name meant "soulful". Soledad didn't learn what her name meant until one day when they were driving up Highway 101 and she saw the name on a sign. She had never heard anyone with the same name and just assumed it was something her mother had dreamed up special just for her. After all, the cousins had strange names—Gug, Peachley, Pris, Mento. Her fifth-grade teacher told her that Soledad was Spanish for alone. Hearing that made her feel cursed in some way.

Once Soledad's mother was dead, the ten-year old was shuffled back and forth between aunts and other relatives, living on roads called Wild Horse Canyon, Mango Grove, Sycamore Lane, Prune Path, and Garlic Field Arroyo. You might say Soledad had a wild agricultural kind of life. She knew how to seed crops, grow crops, harvest crops, irrigate and feed crops before she could multiply. She picked tomatoes and apricots alongside her cousins, getting paid at the end of the day by a man who weighed her pickings. Even though she was small, she usually managed to out-pick her older cousins. Fast and tough. When she walked her body seemed to weave its way through space like a vine growing along an adobe wall, like a quick green lizard shuffling through your basket of laundry.

Soledad blew in and out of people's lives all across the Salinas Valley. By the time she was 19 at least eight men could claim that they had "spent time" with her. She danced in and out, back and forth through her mother's large family who always had open arms for her and called her "the family tragedy" behind her back. And because they saw her in that light, it was what she became. As cursed by their perception of her as she was by her prophetic name. Always alone, Soledad kicked and fought her way into adulthood. Her broken-down cowboy boots said all you needed to know about her—she could scrap her way out of any jam. She clawed, bit, punched, kicked and elbowed her way through life. Until she met Adio.

Adio was a cowhand on a dude ranch, not far from her Uncle Nestor's farm, where she was spending the summer helping with the harvest. Uncle Nestor had a soft spot in his heart for his odd-ball great niece. He let her stay in an old chicken coop that he had converted into a tiny bedroom. It even had an electric line stretched from his house to her coop. He gave her a bed and a mattress and a few old rugs to throw on the floor. When not working, Soledad spent her time reading, watching the birds, braiding together bits of straw and vines that she made into oddly shaped creations which she hung in the windows of her chicken coop room. She was definitely a loner.

The day she first saw Adio, she had brought a bushel of cabbages from Nestor's farm to the dude ranch, a few miles up the road. Pete's Dude Ranch catered to middle income people who mainly lived in the Central Valley. These were basically blue collar down-to-earth people looking for an affordable weekend. Mostly guys who liked to come up with their buddies, drink a shitload of beer, ride horses and play cowboy. Nights spent in the one bar that was about five miles down the road. Loud western music, a few couples dancing. And lots of guys whooping and hollering. Pete's Dude Ranch was known for its Dudalicious Cole Slaw, made from a guarded old family recipe, handed down from Pete's great-grandmother.

Adio had been working at Pete's for about 20 years, since he was 15. He never graduated high school and was good with horses. Knew how to talk them down, knew how to break them. Gently. He was a kind of whisperer, a quiet dude, soft spoken and pretty much a loner. When he saw Soledad carrying in a box of pale green cabbages, he felt like someone had stabbed him through his eye, right into his brain. He heard a distant buzzing sound in his head. He thought he was having a stroke or something. Soledad stopped what she was doing and looked him in the eye. That was it.

Soledad felt herself being swept up in a storm of desire. Adio was 15 years older. His gentle nature and his way with horses fascinated her, as most of the men she knew were hard and mean. He quietly won her heart. For a long time she made daily deliveries of produce to the ranch. They never spoke. They simply watched each other. She admired his boots. She loved the way he put his face right up close to a horse's face, and as if by magic, became able to lead the horse around the corral. Adio knew she was watching him. And she knew he was observing her as she walked back to the pickup. She felt his eyes on her, watching her walk.

He eventually came calling and Uncle Nestor approved of him. Soledad came out of her shell. Their courtship lasted about eight years and then the dude ranch closed. Adio, with no education and dyslexic, had few employable skills. Ranch hand jobs were hard to find and he rambled around the valley doing small jobs. Breaking a difficult colt, patching fences, laying down blacktop, helping build barns. He started hanging around with a rough crowd, drinking too much.

Things between him and Soledad remained tight, but he moved a lot. She settled down in Salinas, working in a coffee shop, earning little money. She remained tough and scrappy. Now, almost 30, Soledad looked worn out. She only softened when Adio came to visit and they spent their time in her tiny apartment listening to Willie Nelson and drinking too much, passing out together. For a few days after each visit, Soledad seemed more relaxed, less defensive, almost smiling at her customers.

Things for Adio turned bad eventually. One night, while drunk, he agreed to drive the getaway car for a home robbery in a fancy home. That the house was in a gated community concerned him, but his buddies swore it was a piece of cake. "That guy at the front gate? Damn. He's a wuss. Besides, he's Antonio's sister's nephew and he knows the plan and we told him we'd cut him in." Adio agreed, although he wasn't so sure he trusted the plan. But what the hell. He was broke and drunk and desperate for money.

Of course, the plan failed. Guns were pulled and shots fired and almost immediately the cops showed up. Flashing lights, sirens, the whole deal. In the end, Adio was convicted as an accomplice and sentenced to serve eight years in Salinas Valley State Prison, located in Soledad, California. Just a few miles from where Soledad lived.

As an inmate in a minimum security prison, Adio had a bit of freedom, not to mention three squares a day. Plus, he got to see Soledad for visitations quite often.

For Soledad, her regular visits to the prison kept her going. Three years had passed and she was used to the drive down Highway 101. She felt like she could almost do it in her sleep. On her way to her last visit to see Adio, she was feeling a bit woozy from too much drinking the night before. She had spent the evening at Barney's Bar, a local hangout with a rough and tumble crowd. She was one of the regulars, known as a tough hothead who thought nothing of getting in people's faces if they said or did something she didn't like. Unfortunately, she wasn't able to sleep it off and awoke with a splitting headache. After drinking a beer, to hopefully do what four aspirin didn't take care of, she started on the road. She had chosen a red long sleeved western shirt that Adio liked. And new denims. Stonewashed and tight, but not too tight to keep them from banning her entrance into the visitor's section. Dressing in a provocative way was not allowed. Touching was only allowed in the beginning of the visit and at the end. Brief moments of physical closeness, which they both relished.

The sky that Sunday morning was grayish, filled with mottled dark clouds. The air felt muggy. Soledad wished the air conditioner in her car was working. She wished she felt better. She wished the traffic would move faster. She was running late and she felt stressed and sick. As she went to pass a slow moving pickup, she neglected to double check her side view mirror. And that's when it happened. A truck driver who was hauling tons of cabbages couldn't stop fast enough to avoid hitting Soledad's vehicle. The crash took her by surprise and in her panic, Soledad swerved her car back and forth between the pickup she was passing and the cabbage truck. It was an impossible situation to avoid. Her car rolled, ending up on its hood. The cabbage truck also tipped over, covering her car with close to a ton of cabbages. By the time a few drivers stopped to help, she was already dead. Her red western shirt had not a wrinkle and her new denims still smelled new. A plastic container of chocolate chip cookies had opened and were strewn all over the back seat. Her 7-Eleven coffee had spilled, splashing on her red tennis shoes.

The headlines in the Salinas Valley newspaper read *Woman Killed by Cabbage Truck*. The driver of the cabbage truck somehow survived and was not charged and the driver of the pickup she was trying to pass, who watched it all through his rear view mirror, ended up going into therapy. He felt somehow responsible.

And Adio? He still has some time to serve. He was allowed to attend a small memorial service for Soledad, wearing chains and handcuffs. No one visits him anymore, although he has a pen pal who lives in Pennsylvania, who claims she is planning to come and visit him in prison. He is still waiting.

Bayard

My old university sends me their alumni magazine every six months. I usually leaf through it, looking for familiar names. Someone was named professor of the year at Harvard, someone else became CEO of a huge corporation, another person had a painting accepted into the Museum of Modern Art. I never recognize any of these names, which makes me wonder. Is it that none of my friends ever amounted to anything (including myself), or perhaps that none of us report our triumphs to the alumni magazine?

When the latest issue arrived I did my customary skimming. I checked the obituaries, which I always do, and saw the name of an old boyfriend. Bayard had passed away. It didn't say how or why. All it said was Bayard Demerchant, '68, followed by a date which might be his date of death or his birthday or a misprint of the day he lead an anti-war demonstration in the middle of campus. Anything seems possible, considering all things.

Bayard was my first brush with exotica. I grew up in a small town, where I was considered exotic myself—I was Jewish. My family brought their New York accents and bohemian ways with them when they moved to a small industrial town in the middle of flat farmland in northeastern Ohio. Known for their involvement in the theatre, their left wing politics. We had homosexual friends.

Bayard was big and dark and mysterious. He walked across campus in a black wool coat, hunched over, smoking cigarettes, looking like a young man with many secrets. Growing up in Spanish Harlem, he had a tough exterior. He appeared to be unapproachable and I watched him for two years, too shy to speak to him. One night a friend introduced us. Bayard made a point of telling me that his father was French and his mother Mexican, not Puerto Rican. It was something he wanted everyone to know—the not Puerto Rican part.

We became friends. On my part, it was a strange kind of hero worship. Bayard was politically outspoken at a time when there was a lot to speak out against. We were both involved in the civil rights and anti-war movement, along with the domestic Peace Corps (VISTA), caught up in our political activities, dabbling occasionally in schoolwork, suspecting we might flunk out of college. To flunk out for involvement in a cause was far superior to flunking out due to stupidity. And we assured each other that neither of us was stupid.

Every night we met at a local pub, drank a few beers and then headed down the road to a tunnel under the train tracks, where we sat on cold rocks and smoked cigarettes. Bayard played the guitar and sang folk songs, political songs, sad Spanish ballads that he never translated for me. I was transfixed watching him, his long fingers moving up and down the neck of his guitar, his dark eyes filling with tears. Sometimes we would kiss and touch each other for hours. Winter in Ohio, especially inside a damp tunnel, can be unforgiving. The frigid air outside and the heat inside my body was exhilarating and Bayard never seemed to be bothered by the cold. His bare hands felt hot against my skin and his mouth warm and soft. I imagined him a wild animal, hungry and yet protective. Eventually, the cold sent us shivering back to our separate rooms.

After I graduated and moved away, Bayard and I lost touch. We never pretended there was any future awaiting us as a couple. We weren't a couple. We just liked to hang out together. There were no promises, no commitments. I desired more stability than he could offer. I eventually got married and moved to another city. After several years, Bayard somehow managed to find me. We spoke on the phone occasionally. He was still living in the town where we had gone to school. Our conversations, generally flat and marginally personal (work, politics, music) usually ended after just a few minutes and it would be months before he would, again, telephone. A few times we met for drinks or dinner in a nearby town, during which the conversation became no more interesting than our phone calls. He wanted to know about my marriage, but only minor details. We talked about his job as a union organizer or mine as a schoolteacher. We reminisced about all our adventures in college.

The last time I saw him, he had invited me to visit him and his new wife and baby. He lived in a cluttered old house with tie-dyed pillows spread across a dilapidated couch, and African masks hanging on the walls. We smoked dope, drank wine, listened to the Doors, and spoke in dreamy voices. We talked politics, the war, Nixon, Cambodia. I knew his wife from college, so she and I swapped stories about mutual acquaintances. They let me hold their new baby and rave about how beautiful she was. It felt good to be together as we remembered and laughed.

When it was time for me to leave, Bayard told me he wanted to show me something. He took me into the bedroom, which smelled of cigarettes and incense. He closed the door and gently pulled me to him and kissed me. His lips were softer than I remembered and it took my breath away. Then he put both of his hands in my long hair, pulling my face into his chest, the way he had done all those nights we made out under the railroad bridge. "Don't forget me," he whispered into my hair. "Just don't ever forget me." On the dresser behind him sat a lava lamp. I watched its illuminated orange blob undulate through heavy oil in its struggle to move and reform itself into a new shape. Bayard smelled of patchouli and damp wool. Shortly after that I moved to California and lost track of him. The other day I found a photograph of him walking down steps on the college campus. Smoking, scowling, his hand raised in an ambivalent wave.

Accidental Clarity

(Rolling Forward on Silent Wheels)

"She thinks about sitting in the store in the evenings.
The light in the street, the complicated reflections
in the windows. The accidental clarity."
Alice Munro, *Differently*

I think about sitting in the store in the evenings. The light in the street, the complicated reflections in the windows. The accidental clarity, as if the world seen through the doubled and tripled-paned surfaces of glass appears more glorious than it does in normal vision. I remember this as I finger the delicate silk of my blouse. It's a color I will always remember, not the blue of a sky illuminated by bright sun, but the blue of the sky taking on the darkness of encroaching night—rich and deep like the sea at sunset. Perhaps the name of the color is indigo. When I saw myself in a mirror wearing this particular blouse, it never failed to astound me that anything I owned, let alone wore against my skin, could be so gorgeous and lush.

"I will never see this color again, will I?" I ask this question aloud, not thinking anyone is in the room.

"I guess not, Sis. Can you remember it?" The sound of her voice surprises me. I am annoyed and don't want to know that she has come close enough to hear my softly spoken words. Since losing my eyesight I speak to myself, as if I am now two different people—the one who remembers and the one who listens to the memories.

"Of course I remember. Blindness doesn't take away memory of sight. You should know that. Haven't you and Joey gone to those classes? Didn't they tell you that?" I know that her comment was meant to be kind. I am merciless and don't care. I suspect she is sleeping with my husband behind my back. Of course, I have never come out directly and asked her. It is something I assume, something I sense in the same way I sense Joey's moods before he walks in the room.

"Oh, yes. I did know that, but was just wondering..."

"You think that because I can't see, that I don't know what goes on around here?" There is a long silence and I sense my sister shift nervously inside her clothing. I can hear the fabric slide across her skin.

"I was just asking, Sis. I didn't mean to offend you." Now I am ashamed of myself. She offered to come and take care of me until I can get adjusted to sightlessness. I am an ungrateful bitter blind woman. We both know that Joey doesn't have the patience. We both know that he will leave me as soon as he believes I can manage on my own. I know that he will leave us both in the end.

Later, as we walk down the street, my sister tells me what is in all the store windows. Her arm is bent at the elbow, her forearm crossing her waist, and I hold on to her upper arm with my right hand. She has a way of gliding down the street as if she is standing on large soft wheels that roll gently forward. I have never been able to walk like this. I bounce and jolt and change pace, depending on what catches my attention. Until now, that is. Now I must settle myself to her slow. steady, floating pace. It is reassuring.

"Oh look" (she always says this to me and then mutters "I'm sorry, Sis"). This is something I can forgive and just squeeze her arm to let her know it's okay. "It's a whole display of Elvis Presley records and some black leather jackets and cowboy boots. And lots of pictures of Elvis playing the guitar." We have stopped, apparently, in front of Nichol's Music store. I am told that someday I will know where I am by recognizing small rises and bumps in the sidewalk, by the sounds that come out of the different stores, by the flow of traffic on the street, by the smells of surrounding restaurants and business establishments. I can't imagine that I will ever be able to do that. I sniff the air and notice the faint odor of shoe polish and glue. Then I remember that Frankie's Shoe Repair shop is just a few doors down from Nichol's. I wonder if this is evidence of progress. My sister hums "Love Me Tender" in her high thin voice.

Joey, getting into bed, pulls me gently out of a soft semi-sleep. He is supposed to help me get ready for bed until I learn where to find my toothbrush, pajamas, how to put my clothes away so that I don't trip over them when I get out of bed. Before blindness I was a slob, but now it is imperative that everything be put in its place. My sister stayed late to help me to bed because Joey never came home. I don't remember hearing her leave.

"Hey Babe. How's it goin'?" Joey, persistently cheerful, acts as if I have come down with a cold. "Feeling better today?" We don't talk about what has happened. He says things like "OK, you can do this." His voice gets louder at the end, like a high school coach sending the team in for the last grueling quarter. "Do what?" I ask, simply to get him to perhaps address that what I am doing is learning how to live without sight. It's like being born into a new body that remembers everything but can't find where the hell it is.

"Oh, you know. The whole thing. You can do this. I know you can." That is always his answer. Even when we go to see the counselor at the Braille Institute, Joey is silent. I can hear him breathing beside me, clearing his throat nervously. His hand, always holding mine, trembles slightly. After 23 years together, I know him. He is scared.

He pushes my hair back from my face. The calloused palms of his hands brush against my forehead. I will never forget how they look—the squatness, the scars that cross his left hand, the nails like flat shovels, pink and healthy. He loves to fiddle with my hair, which used to be long and silky. I have no idea how it looks anymore. I had it cut, but don't remember how long ago it was.

Living in darkness, without seeing the transition between day and night, makes it difficult for me to keep track of time. I experience time differently now. It seems to flow smoothly without the old familiar stops and starts imposed by clocks, sunlight, moonlight. It is like swimming in tepid water all the time, floating in nothingness. I wake up from a nap and have no idea what time it is, how long I've been asleep, where I am. My universe is now dark and timeless. I will never see my skin wrinkle, my hair turn gray, my breasts droop any farther than they did when I lost my sight four months ago. I touch my body all the time now, seeking its familiarity. It is reassuring to luxuriate in the pleasure of my own skin. "Why are you so late?" I ask.

"I'm not that late, Babe. Really. It's only about 11." He knows I can't check on him. We still haven't bought a Braille clock I can read with my hands. "I had to balance the books and stock shelves, then I stopped at Jack's Pub for a beer with the guys." That explains the smell of mint on his breath. "I couldn't wait to come home and see you." I would give anything in the world to believe this is true. I would give away the last ten years of my life to feel in my heart that Joey felt that way, just for tonight. "Your little sis is waiting for me to take her home, honey. Is it okay if I drive her back to her place? It's late." When he talks about her this way it sounds like she is 13 years old and incapable of taking a taxi.

"Joey, my "little sis" is almost 39. She's not a child. She has a name, you know. Remember?"

"Damn. Don't start now. I'm tired. I know her name and I am just trying to be polite by driving Serena home after she spent the day here helping you. Excuse me for trying to be nice. Excuuuuuse me."

I don't know how much time has passed. I must have fallen asleep. The house is silent and I know that I am in the bed alone. I have to pee, and get out of bed, practicing what I have learned— feel the edge of the bed, swing my feet over the side, orient myself by remembering what the room looks like, where the door is, stand up and count the steps as I walk forward holding my hands out in front of me, waving them slightly back and forth so I don't walk into anything. Joey is famous for leaving doors partially open. I feel my way down the hallway to where I know the bathroom is. The thick carpeting hushes all the sounds I make. I feel like a ghost floating through a house. Unseen. Something about blindness makes me feel invisible. I have no idea what I look like, if I have green stuff in my teeth, if my hair is sticking up all over the place, if I have dirt on my face, if my clothes match. I would prefer to be invisible.

"We can't do this anymore." These are words I hear whispered. I don't know where they're coming from—perhaps from the second bedroom, perhaps from the living room. "I have a feeling she knows."

"You're crazy. How could she know? She's blind, for Christ's sake."

"She said something today. It scared me."

"Like, what did she say that scared you?"

"She said something about how she knows what's going on around here. I just think we should cool it."

"Well, maybe you're right. Come on, Serena, once more for old time's sake. It'll be the last time ever, OK?"

"You said that last time. I don't believe you anymore."

"Shit. I promise. Really, I do. She doesn't know anything. But you're right. This is wrong and we'll just have to stop. But just one more... oh honey, I just gotta touch you here. Just one more time..." The sound of rustling sheets and soft sighs and the movement of skin against skin threads through the silent air.

For a moment I feel dizzy, disoriented. That I am blind has escaped me for an instant and I keep trying to open my eyes even wider, believing that I will then be able to get my bearings. I float down the hall like Serena does, rolling forward on silent wheels. Feeling for the edge of my bed, I trip and fall clumsily on top of it.

Some time later Joey slides under the sheets. His body emanates an unfamiliar warmth that I now understand. I listen to him breathing evenly until I know he's asleep. Slowly I roll to his side of the bed and spoon my body behind his, tucking my knees into the fold of his legs. I breathe deeply, like a bloodhound following a scent. The odor of sex and guilt whispers inside my nose. I slide my arm under his neck and tighten myself against his back. So familiar, this skin, this shoulder, this long bumpy spine against my stomach. I lick his shoulder, which carries a suggestion of something salty. I think about his face and I can see it in my mind, which is different from having a memory of sight. This face is simply here before me, more familiar than anything in my world, as if my sight has returned. I touch my eyes and they are closed. Yet I see his eyes, his forehead, his round cheeks, crooked teeth. He is as familiar to me as I am to myself. Perhaps more.

Joey's breathing is deep and nasal as he twitches slightly, releasing tension. I suppose he's got a lot to release these days. My heart flutters with anger and compassion and I wonder how this is possible. And then he moans in his sleep.

Naked Tomatoes

Ohio, in the summer, is green and moist. Fine droplets of sweat trickle down your neck. Sometimes you can feel sweat creeping down the small of your back and when your shirt touches your skin the cloth turns cool and wet, making you shiver in spite of the oppressive heat; a strange kind of magic.

In the mid 1950's life is idyllic on the surface. The war over, the boys home and everyone is making babies in the post-war frenzy of horniness and relief. Women in our enclave of a neighborhood are doing exactly what they imagine they are supposed to be doing: creating picture perfect homes filled with gingham curtains and General Electric appliances—all the things they dreamed of during their Depression era childhoods. Prim and tucked in, isolated in their kitchens baking pies, frying chicken, reading Betty Crocker cookbooks, watching the clock over the kitchen sink and waiting for their husbands to walk through the front door after work.

During these sticky summer months, once a week in the late afternoon, a man comes down the road with a wagon pulled by a geriatric horse. He parks the wagon in the middle of the block, right in front of our house, and rings a crude brass bell. They call him "The Italian." I don't think anyone knows his name. Swarthy and exotic with a small mustache, oiled hair and muscled arms, he smiles as he watches the neighborhood women saunter down the road. His wagon is piled with bushels of fresh produce. You can hear wooden screen doors open and slam shut. The hinges are rusted from the cold winters and damp summers and each door groans and squeaks like a woman in pain. A woman in pleasure.

The Italian leans against the side of the wagon smoking a cigarette as he observes the group of women approaching him, like wilted flowers staggered along the road. In his mind, he clicks off their names and any other information he can remember about them. The redhead, Susie Pink, usually carries a cranky child on her hip and likes only the corn with the tiny kernels. The old one in the black hairnet (Mrs. Pinter) prefers the longest thinnest cucumbers. The fat one with the flushed face and toothy smile likes her peaches soft. She is Dora. He knows that my mother prefers red peppers over the green ones, that she always buys three bunches of scallions. He knows that she waits until the other women have gone home before she comes outside to select her produce.

Neatly dressed, he smells faintly of cologne and perspiration. Shoes shined, pleated pants hanging loosely over his small frame, he wears a clean white shirt, sleeves rolled up, the top four buttons left undone. His suspenders are as dark as the hair on his chest. He bows slightly and tips a rakish black hat, charming in that old European way.

The women speak loudly to him, as though he were hard of hearing. Some of them talk slowly to make sure that he understands them, while others are in a hurry to get back to their kitchens. Some women, usually the younger ones, take their time, ask how his family is, pat his old horse on the neck. Some women bring him things—a bottle of Coke, a carrot for the horse, a bag of cookies to take home, a sandwich wrapped in wax paper. The others watch with knowing looks. "There she goes again," they snicker to each other. "Can't keep her eyes offa him." Several of the women are attracted to the Italian, but they would never admit it. They are, after all, trying to convince themselves that this quiet small town life is all they had ever dreamed of. Exotica is not a part of the picture and as everyone knows, women who have dreams of an intriguing life are the ones who are never quite content with what they have.

The Italian waits patiently as they approach. Eyes glazed from heat and humidity, tiny pools of perspiration standing in the curve above their upper lips. He gazes now and then at their mouths—those soft plums.

Some of the women wear cotton housedresses, aprons still tied around their waists, revealing full hips and bottoms as round as melons. The colors and patterns remind him of fields of flowers from his childhood in the hills above Naples—all swaying motion and color. The older women wear dark dresses and laced shoes. The fine lines that radiate around their eyes and the soft loosening skin under their jaw lines fascinate him. Their tailored dresses are fastened down the front with shiny black buttons, some with a glass bead or rhinestone in the middle. He sometimes allows his eyes to linger just a little too long on those buttons. Rumors swirl around the neighborhood regarding which Mrs. So-and-So was ogled. "The nerve of him, that Italian. Did you see him stare?" The ogled ones act outraged, but most of them are secretly flattered. My mother isn't like the other women. If there is ogling to be done, it will be a private affair.

There had not been time enough to forget that the Italians sided with Hitler at the beginning of the war. They mistrust (on principle), but are intrigued with this dark man who speaks with a thick accent. He can recognize each one of them by the fragrance they exude—mothballs, rotting flowers, garlic, cinnamon, breast milk, shampoo, violet toilet water, bleach and perspiration.

In spite of all this and because of all this the women still float down the street to him each time they hear the clang of his bell. His produce is fresh and cheap and most of them don't drive and it is too damn hot to walk the three miles to the nearest grocer. Some of the housewives are shy and almost afraid to look into his face. Mary Jane Murphy is usually so nervous that she wraps her finger through her hair until pins fall out and she is left with hanks of it flopping around her thin pale face. She speaks with a thick southern drawl which makes it difficult for him to understand her. "Misses, you wanta chipotes? The onions? No? I'ma sorry, Misses.

Did you say no? Deesa melons? Is a nica too, deesa melons. You want?"

Some of the women like to touch the produce before they buy it. My mother touches, squeezes, tastes and smells. Mrs. Beck never buys anything from the Italian until she samples it. She snaps a carrot and takes a bite, cracks a few beans and holds them up to the light to see how moist and fresh they are. She squeezes and sniffs his apricots and eyes him suspiciously, asking him to repeat the price, which is already printed on a chalk board. Mrs. Beck is Italian herself, a fact that she has managed to keep hidden from the other women on the street, thanks to the miracle of peroxide and a rinse called Golden Glow.

The Italian isn't fooled by Mrs. Beck's bleached hair. Her dark brows and black Sicilian eyes give her away, along with the defiance with which she approaches him. Italiana, he thinks to himself. He recognizes the same suspicious look that he sees in his wife's eyes when she accuses him of holding back money at the end of a day so he can buy Chianti.

I am ten years old and secretly watch all of this, every week, from an ancient glider on our long front porch. It is one of my rituals, along with counting caterpillars, sneaking candy from the drawer where my mother thinks she is hiding it, and searching under my parents' bed for used rubbers. I don't know what they are or what they are used for, but I know I am not supposed to touch them. Therefore, they are my enthrallment.

Of all the women, the one who fascinates me the most is Rhona who lives at the end of the street. The neighbors claim that she sunbathes in her backyard naked. Small and curvaceous, she wears tight toreador pants and ruffled off-the-shoulder peasant blouses. Rhona prances right up to the Italian, keeping her face very close to his as she tells him what she wants. Sometimes she hands him a cold bottle of Coke before she takes her small packages, places them in a string bag and strolls up the street, her hips swaying side to side. The Italian's eyes follow her, even when another woman is speaking to him. When Rhona gets to the end of the block, she always turns and waves to him, seeming to know that his eyes are still on her.

My mother's main chore every summer, besides dabbling at housework, is to attain and maintain a beautiful tan. She spends hours lying on a lounge chair in the backyard, where she torments her sun darkened skin on a daily basis. Slathered in olive oil, she flips from front to back like a hamburger, until I imagine I can hear a faint sizzling sound. Then she goes upstairs to take a bubble bath and comes down fresh and sparkling, her long legs polished with lotion, toenails painted slick and shiny, smelling of Chanel #5.

One day, after watching the scene on the road, I come inside to play solitaire at the kitchen table. On this particular day, the radio is on. My mother and I listen to Guy Lombardo and Benny Goodman, Bartok and Rachmaninoff. When my mother hears the Italian's bell ring the second time, to notify the women that he is about to leave, she rinses her hands in water and runs her palms along the sides of her head, attempting to smooth back her hair, which she wears in a ponytail, replacing pins to catch the long wisps of dark hair that dangle down her neck and around her face.

My mother never rushes and her gestures are deliberate, as though moving through water. Methodically, she unties her apron and places it carefully on the back of a dining room chair. She usually wears shorts in the summer; she is the only woman on the block who dresses like this—shorts and a thin sleeveless blouse. Her nut-colored skin is dark against the white of her blouse and her dangling earrings show off her long neck. My father complains that there are too many vegetables and tells her to stop buying until we have eaten what's "in there." He is referring, of course, to the refrigerator, which seems to be an appliance that frightens him. When he asks my mother to get him a cold beer she asks him why he doesn't get it for himself. He responds that he doesn't like to go "in there." Maybe he's afraid of all those vegetables.

I follow my mother into the front room. She gets her purse out of the closet, takes some bills and pushes them down into her pocket. After checking to see that all her small white buttons are fastened, she dabs on pearly pink lipstick, grabs a cigarette and walks onto the front porch. My mother is the only woman on the street who smokes in public. I follow behind her to the Italian's produce cart.

By now the other women are gone, having returned to their hot kitchens, hungry children and soon-to-return husbands. My mother walks across the road, around the outside of the cart, picking up peaches and plums, holding a bunch of grapes in the bowl of her manicured fingers. She hands her items to the Italian, who places them in small brown bags as she makes her way through the green leafy spinach and the red-veined chard. She sniffs the nectarines with her eyes closed and nods her head at him. "Hmmm. These smell good." The Italian watches her, glancing down at her red toenails and sandaled feet. I talk to the horse for a few minutes and feed him a carrot but soon grow bored and return to the house, where I doze off on the couch in the front room.

Suddenly I am awake with that slightly nauseated feeling, the result of an afternoon nap. I want my mother but don't hear her in the house. I look out the front window and see the horse and cart standing in the road. Alone. I search the house and realize she's not here and decide to continue my search to the backyard. Walking down the flagstone steps behind the garage, I notice my mother and the Italian in her garden. This is the year my mother has tried to grow corn. The Italian is tenderly pulling back one of the leaves and with his broad fingers, picks something off the stalk and holds it out to my mother to inspect.

"Misses, thisa thing will eat your corn." He sweeps his arm, indicating the entire garden. "Is gotta have some water." He points to her bare feet and shakes his head disapprovingly. He bends down and carefully brushes away stalks of weeds and grass. When he stands up, his hand grazes his crotch, which my mother notices and turns her head to take a final puff from her cigarette before she tosses it to the ground.

They move to the tomatoes, which are growing along the fence. The neighbor on the other side of the fence is an old widow who never smiles and calls us "Kikes." My parents told me she is German, as though they were announcing she had the plague. The Italian bends over one of the vines. I watch him pick off a crimson globe and split it open, placing one half in his mouth and the other into my mother's waiting hand. She takes small bites and the seeds fall against her brown chest and down the front of her blouse. He watches my mother—her body, her face, her hands, her long narrow feet. He watches her mouth as she chews the tomato. He picks another one and begins to peel away the soft skin until he is left holding a skinless tomato in the crest of his fingers, which he offers to her. "You see, Misses, she no is dressed. We eat her like a deez in Italy. You try? Manga. Manga." My mother reaches out to take the peeled fruit but she doesn't put it in her mouth. Maybe she is thinking about my father or the chicken that's sitting in a bowl on the linoleum counter in the kitchen. Maybe she's afraid to eat this peeled thing. Maybe she's wondering where I am. I don't make a peep.

When she finally closes her eyes and takes a deep sucking bite out of the pink flesh, the seeds squirt out and she starts to laugh. The Italian chuckles along with her and the two of them just stand there giggling. Then the Italian searches his pocket for two cigarettes, which he lights, offering one to my mother. They smoke in silence for a minute or two and then, as if they had rehearsed it in a play, they each throw their cigarettes over the fence into the neighbor's yard.

Not wanting to be seen, I return to the house, where I flip on T.V. and try to get lost in the Mousketeers. I am so hot and sweaty that my legs stick to the chair and my back is soaking wet and feels chilled against the tangerine tinted Naugahyde. A slight breeze moves through the open windows. I hear screen doors open and close, cars driving slowly up the street. The men are starting to come home from work. By the angle of shafts of sunlight shining through the dining room window, I can tell that my father will be home soon. He'll be sweaty and droopy after driving all day in his delivery truck, smelling of cigarettes, automotive supplies and sweat. He'll drink a beer out on the front porch, have a few smokes and read the paper before he goes upstairs to take a shower. After dinner he will probably take me out for frozen custard.

At some point I hear my mother and the Italian walking up the driveway toward the road. When I get off the chair, my skin sticks to it and then pulls away, like a huge Band-Aid being ripped from the back of my thighs. I watch them through the side window, where I can look down at my mother's body. Her face is narrow and her nose looks larger than it really is. Her breasts are like the front of an airplane without the propeller. They stick straight out and I think I can see the Italian's eyes glancing at them occasionally.

Most of the time he seems to be looking at her mouth. He is speaking to her, softly, haltingly, his voice hushed and low. I can't hear his words. My mother nods her head and brushes the wet strands of hair off the back of her neck. Her blouse has become unbuttoned at the top and there is a pale pink tomato stain right down the middle. They each have a cigarette and their exhaled smoke forms a faint cloud around their faces. At the end of the driveway, my mother turns to come into the house and the Italian walks out to his old horse and his vegetable cart.

My mother comes into the house, shaking her white blouse back and forth to cool herself. Her face is flushed and her eyes glazed, the way they look in the morning when she first wakes up. I notice that her lips look swollen. She touches her finger to her mouth and goes to look at herself in the mirror on the door of the coat closet. She leans closer to get a better view of her lips before she puts on more silvery pink lipstick.

"God damn. It's hot out there." She starts to walk back into the kitchen. Her feet are dirty from the garden and she looks at me.

"Where have you been?" she asks casually.

"Oh, playing solitaire and watching Mousketeers. Annette's boobies are getting bigger, Mom." I try to act normal.

"Uh huh. Boobies do that. What else were you doing?"

"Nothing, really. I think I fell asleep on the couch. What's for dinner?" I think she's convinced. She rattles off a list of food items, adding that she bought peaches from The Italian.

When my father comes home, we eat baked chicken and plates of corn and cucumber wedges. In a cracked bowl my mother has sliced peeled tomatoes sprinkled with green onions and vinegar. My father mentions that the tomatoes are different and asks her what she has done to them.

"I peeled them, like they do in Italy." My mother avoids my father's eyes and takes a swallow from her tall glass of iced black coffee.

"Naked tomatoes. Well, how do you like that?" My father smiles, first at me and then at my mother, as he hoists a delicate tomato slice in the air for our approval. I can tell he likes them because he finishes the bowl himself. My mother picks at her food, claiming that it's too hot to eat. I keep looking at her mouth, which by now looks normal.

After dinner I watch my father bring the dishes over to the sink, where my mother washes them. She has forgotten to put on her apron and the water has sloshed all the way down her front. Each time my father hands her another plate, he touches her somewhere—her breast, her ass, her upper arm. When he kisses the back of her neck, she shivers slightly and then turns toward him and tells him to stop bothering her. She smiles now and her voice is warm and deep, like whiskey. My father turns toward me and brushes his hands in my direction, shooing me out of the kitchen and then turns back to my mother, sliding his body behind her, lifting the wisps of hair off the back of her neck. Around her feet is a small puddle of muddy water.

Yola Wears Tennis Shoes

"Write big," she yells at me. "Bigger." This is my grandmother. She sits behind me, watching me make words on a white board.

We call her Yola, me and my sisters. She is the mother of my step-father. Yola Thundercloud. She is short and round, like a pumpkin. When she was a child, girls on the Pueblo didn't go to school. She learned to build pots and decorate them, glaze them, cook them in the small round horno behind the hut. Then she learned to sit in the square in Taos and sell them. She is tough, my Yola. No gringo can swindle her. Once she told them to go fuck themselves and was asked not to come back.

So now she wants me to teach her to write. I mark my letters on the white board with a pen that smells like whiskey. First I taught her to print and now I am teaching her cursive.

We live in the Pueblo. Our house was built about 500 years ago. When I go into Taos I see new buildings with flat walls and sharp corners, houses with trees and flowers. On the Pueblo, the only green we see is patches of corn. Our adobes are connected, like a family afraid to leave each other. My Yola says we are all one together and if we separate we will not be able to stand. She tells me that our people have lived here for thousands of years.

"There, Yola. What did I write?" Yola squints. "The capitol of New Mexico is Santa Te."

"It says Santa Fe!"

"Well, it looks like Santa Te to me. Is that an F or a T?" She knows it's an F. I erase the F and write a better one.

31

"Santa Fe" she reads in a booming voice. She grunts and pulls herself off her chair. Her bent old body moves close to the white board nailed to the wall. With her left arm she sticks out her pointer finger and traces the shape of the words. Her hand shakes and she has to bend and tilt and shuffle to the right as she follows the swirls and curves of my letters.

"The E starts on the other side" I tell her. Yola acts like she doesn't hear me. She doesn't like to be wrong about anything. She has never tried to write. She simply traces my writing. She brushes her hands together as if she is the one who wrote it in the first place.

At night Yola pulls the blanket over me and my twin sister. Her brown face is lined with deep wrinkles and there is a bucket of skin under each eye. I think she is beautiful like this. She has looked this way as long as I can remember. Yola wears tennis shoes—white ones. My mother buys them for her at Walmart.

"You did that great, Yola." I take a little gold star and stick it on the back of her hand. Yola beams at me. She calls me her little teacher and scrunches up her nose and pulls me into her big soft breasts and belly. She smells like an onion.

Marcia in Black Panties

The address on the census form reads 5800 Vista Canyon Road, Space 101. I approach a late-model single-wide mobile home and knock on the screen of the sliding glass door. I know someone is home because I hear water running. I look inside and see a short round woman washing dishes in a red tee shirt and black panties. She comes to the door as if she is used to receiving guests in her underwear. She tells me her name is Marcia and she seems very cordial, making some comments about how she tried to fill in the census forms, but it was a long form and she doesn't like all those questions. The long form is about 12 pages and asks for personal information, which, in my opinion, the government already has access to.

My census supervisor has informed me that this woman was rude and hostile to the previous two enumerators, unwilling to give any information. We call these people "refusers" and they gum up the works. I have been chased down the street, had hoses turned on me and had more doors slammed in my face than I can count. When approaching "refusers," we have been trained to be very polite and cautious. As usual, I sympathize, telling her I understand her feelings and that I will be as quick as possible.

"Well, okay. I guess. But make it fast." I must have caught her at a good time. She suddenly disappears and I am not sure what is going on until another sliding glass door on my left opens. She is apparently in another room. Marcia looks down at her panties and seems marginally surprised. "Oh dear," she says nonchalantly.

"Well, I guess it's okay, seeing as how you're a woman."

She answers most of the questions in a clipped tone, as if she is in a hurry to get somewhere. She is 58 and her husband Paul is 80. They have lived in this mobile home for almost 15 years, since moving here from Chicago. Their monthly gas and electric runs about $70. They own one car. They are both Caucasian. They claim no ethnicity. Every so often she makes a comment about her husband being sick, being rushed to the hospital, how stressful it is for her to work with all this going on. Marcia talks so fast that I miss parts of the conversation. I am afraid that perhaps she has mentioned that her husband died and I didn't respond appropriately.

Marcia was born in New York and her husband in Michigan. Her hair is dark and curly and she has a New York accent. She refuses to tell me where she works, but says Paul has been retired for a long time. She gets annoyed when I come to the question about income and I reassure her that she can refuse to answer. She seems a little relieved but still tense, like a racehorse waiting for the gates to open. The sliding glass door is pulled back just far enough for Marcia to squeeze one part of her body sideways onto the porch. She is a woman cut in half.

I ask as few questions as possible. Wanting to make sure I have a correct head count for this address (which is, as far as I'm concerned, all the government really needs to know), I ask her where her husband is now, still thinking she might have told me he died.

"He's in the living room," she says with great annoyance. Like, what are you? Stupid? I turn to look through the other screen door and see Paul sitting in a wheelchair in front of the TV. He is wretchedly thin and pale, with a frayed gray stocking cap pulled down over his fragile head. His eyes meet mine and I wave at him and call out hello. He smiles and tries to wave at me. His right hand is bent at the wrist, his finger twisted. I can tell that the wave is a great effort for him. I see something in Paul's eyes. A question or a plea, as if he wants to talk but has lost the ability to give voice to words, or is perhaps simply too weak to vocalize. He is wearing flannel pajamas and old leather slippers, like my father used to wear. His nose is a hawk's beak against the hollowness of his cheeks. His once blue eyes are washed out and haunting. I am unable to imagine what he looked like as a younger man.

I do the subtraction in my head and compute that Paul is twenty-two years older than Marcia. When she was ten, he was thirty-two. When she was 30, he was 52. Now, the difference in their ages (58 and 80) seems as vast as it was when she was a young child and he was already an adult. Or perhaps it's the fact that she is standing here in her black silk panties, so full of life while he sits strapped in his chair unable to communicate, that makes the age discrepancy so glaring. All I know is that this picture somehow saddens me. Perhaps I have put myself in Marcia's place and know how difficult it would be for me to be in her panties. Or his, for that matter.

Once all the required questions have been answered, Marcia spends about five more minutes chattering at full speed about all kinds of things. She tells me about her car problems, complains about the government (what else is new?), lists all the medications that Paul is taking. She asks my advice about the pots of dying plants that line her tiny front porch. Then, without warning, she abruptly tells me she has to go, squeezes her body back into the room and pulls the screen door shut. As I walk down the steps of the mobile home I can hear her back at the sink banging pots and pans. Walking to my car through the winding narrow road of the mobile home park, I watch the sky darken in minute degrees as evening approaches. I can't get Paul's pleading eyes out of my head.

That night I experience a collage of dreams that fade into oblivion once I am fully awake, except for one image that sticks with me all throughout the following day. In this dream, a couple dances the tango. The music is slow and sensual. Sad and compelling. They dance by me, dressed in black, easily shifting positions, twirling and twirling and then almost crashing into each other. Never losing a beat. Eyes locked on each other. I realize that the man is Paul—a younger virile Paul. I catch a glimpse of the woman he is dancing with. Clearly, without any doubt, I realize that I am his dance partner. I watch Paul and myself float from one end of the room to the other and back again. His pale blue eyes still plead, but this time, with a devilish smile on his lips.

The Ladder

She had heard so many stories about people eloping, her head swimming with images of girls climbing down ladders and falling into the arms of young men, who drove them across state lines to get married. All of these girls looked like Doris Day or Sandra Dee—blond and beautiful and WASP. The cars were convertibles, it was summer, and the guys driving the car always wore button-down shirts.

Of course, Stanley would never have thought of it. He was too engrossed in his studies—his calculus and physics. How could anyone love all those numbers, or be so excited about the prospect of velocity? Boy stuff, Ruthie told herself. She knew she would have to take matters into her own hands.

She wasn't planning to elope, actually. Stanley hadn't yet proposed. In fact, Stanley hadn't asked her out on a date. Not yet. She knew it was just a matter of time and she had already decided that when she and Stanley became involved, she would be the one to run the show. Stanley was like Einstein, who had to be reminded to eat and walked home every day for lunch and supper. She would be Mrs. Einstein, guiding her beloved genius through his daily existence, spoon feeding him, helping him dress. pushing him in the direction of his laboratory and then fetching him at the end of the day.

The ladder conveniently appeared three days ago when Stanley's parents hired two men to paint the outside of their house. Ruthie watched from her bedroom window. She waited patiently as the ladder made its way across the front of the two-story colonial, around the west side and finally came to rest just outside Stanley's bedroom window. The trim around his window had been scraped, and she knew in another 24 hours it would be painted and the ladder would be moved to another location.

She had to act now. Her intention was to get Stanley's attention. Her plan was that, when he saw her standing on a ladder outside his bedroom window, it would bring up thoughts of eloping, marriage, family; and once that seed was planted in his brain, it would just be a matter of time until he realized he wanted to take her to the senior prom. It was already April. A girl couldn't wait till the last minute to plan these things.

Tuesday night Ruthie didn't sleep a wink. She lay in bed and watched the darkness collect in the corners of her room, listening to the song of night air circling inside her lungs. At 3:00 am, when she detected the sound of her father snoring down the hall, she locked herself in the bathroom, where she applied and reapplied her makeup, examining the results in the mirror. She dusted green eye shadow from her lashes all the way up to her eyebrows, hoping it would make her boring dark eyes look green and exotic when seen through Stanley's smudged window. She changed her mind and did the same with blue, realizing she would rather appear to have blue eyes.

Ruthie decided to wear her baby blue flannels under her new pink robe. They were not yet stained with menstrual blood. She wanted to appear as if the whole thing had been unplanned, like a sleepwalking episode. She had rehearsed, for hours, the surprised look on her face, as she pretended to suddenly awaken from a semi-slumber, to find herself on a ladder outside Stanley's window. In her fantasy, Stanley would become alarmed that she might fall off the ladder, and guide her drowsy body into his room, sit her on the bed, pull a blanket around her to keep her warm. She rehearsed walking in the somnambulist way she had seen in movies—that floating movement, the confused look on her face, her blue-appearing eyes blinking in shy surprise. She stood in front of the mirror and repeated "where am I?" with an innocent shocked look on her face. At the last minute she rubbed a bit of rouge across her cheeks.

As she climbed the ladder, chilly air crept up the legs of her pajamas, raising goose bumps on her thighs. When she reached his window, she saw that Stanley's bed was against the far wall— the floor covered with books, clothes, papers, 45 records and slide rules. Stanley, buried under several brown blankets, exposed one pale foot. The bones of his ankle looked delicate, easily fractured. Cautiously, she rapped on the window—once, twice, thrice. No response. Again she rapped, this time using her knuckles, making more noise, and when he didn't respond she resorted to pounding. Stanley scratched himself somewhere under the blankets and his hand shot out to pick his nose in his sleep. Getting frustrated, Ruthie pounded three more times on the window. Stanley refused to wake up. In her anger she shouted "Fuck you, Stanley," and almost toppled over the side of the ladder.

Once Ruthie regained her balance and straightened out the many layers of flannel she was wearing, she realized she had no choice. Feeling hot and somehow embarrassed she began to slowly back down the ladder. Her legs trembled as she cautiously felt for each rung with the toe of her fuzzy zebra-striped slipper. By the time she got back into her bedroom she was sweating and cursing. It had been a stupid idea, hadn't it, she told herself. Stanley was a creep. He was too ugly to be the father of her future children anyway.

Back in her bedroom, Ruthie opened the drawer of her nightstand and unfolded a green sheet of paper with a list of names. Potential Prom Dates was printed in neat block letters across the top. Under the first name, Stanley Grawalski, she had made a short list, each item numbered:

1. lives next door...
2. honor roll...
3. kind of creepy and skinny...
4. doesn't know I exist...

5. never had a girlfriend...

6. the odds—70% chance he'll ask me to the prom if I can get him to notice me...

With a black felt-tipped pen, she put a cross through Stanley's name and made a star by the next name.

Darnell Jackson:

1. black and beautiful...

2. taller than me...

3. great teeth...

4. likes white girls...

5. my father would have a cow....

6. the odds—57% chance he'll ask me to the prom if he breaks up with that bitch Cheryl Spivey...

Ruthie, after shucking off her robe, climbed into bed to dream up her next strategy.

Attempting Flight
Prologue

The stewardess demonstrated how to buckle our seat belts and how to put the oxygen mask over our faces. From her blank expression, it was obvious she had gone through this demonstration about 400 times. She walked down the aisle, pointing to the emergency exits, while looking straight ahead toward the back of the plane as if in a trance. No one paid any attention.

I fiddled with the light above my head, then rummaged through my purse for a piece of gum and found the envelope—the announcement of my father's funeral, containing directions to the church and cemetery, written in turquoise ink by the woman my father was living with when he died. "I am so sorry to inform you that your father passed away last Thursday evening. There will be a funeral on Saturday, June 12th at noon. I know he would have wanted you and your mother to be there. I will be sending her an invitation also. I hope you can make it on such short notice. I would have telephoned, but your father only had your mailing address in his book."

The pilot pulled the jet into position on the runway. The engines roared for half a minute before the plane ever moved. Finally we rolled forward, picking up speed, eventually barreled down the tarmac. The wheels remained on the ground for what seemed like forever. As always, when I am in a plane just taking off, my hands pulled up on the arm rests, as if by my strength alone I could get the huge machine to lift off into the sky. As always, under my breath, I whispered—lift me, lift me!

Several hours later, after dozing off and on, I looked down as the plane crossed the various mountain ranges that separate the West from the bulk of the country. I saw tiny isolated communities sprinkled across parched valleys and mesas, tucked in arroyos, scattered like beads along lengthy stretches of two-lane highways. With all our family's moves and relocations, we had probably settled in a few of those clustered isolated places. There had been so many that I lost count, but certain events from a particular time and place lulled me into a river of memories...

The summer of 1978 I am 14, with long legs and budding breasts, slipping from that filmy envelope of fantasy and innocence into the arresting atmosphere of adolescence. I have been living in the soft cocoon of my parent's world, but am beginning to feel choked, suffocated.

My best friend Lola and I share a fantasy, which we spent the entire school year plotting and planning. After consulting several books on aerodynamics and jet engines, we believe that living so close to the local airfield, we could be lifted into the updraft of one of the jets that swoop over our houses. In the beginning, it was a wild experiment; a daily ritual steeped in fantasy and fairytales, but as the summer progresses, the idea congeals in my heart and I find myself obsessed with escaping my life. Our childlike fantasy had turned into my own private passionate obsession.

Dusty hot winds blow in from the desert, like the devil's oven. Overcome by restlessness, what used to represent comfort and safety (the quiet predictability of each day, each season) has become stifling. I feel like I am living in a small box, tethered to a sparse landscape in the middle of nowhere. I stole a copy of <u>Alice in Wonderland</u> from the local library and cut out the illustration of Alice with her blond hair and huge eyes, a look of surprised anguish on her face, as her head, arm and legs poke through windows of a house much too small for her body. Her expression describes what I feel inside. Whereas Alice has drunk a magic potion, I feel like my own body is fermenting something deep inside me.

Blistering days spread across my horizon and I fear that I will die of boredom. My parents feel restless also. I can tell. They bicker more than usual and my father stays out late at night. My mother watches a lot of TV, smokes too many cigarettes. She waits a lot. I hear less murmuring between them at night, more harsh words and staccato voices. "You know, I waited up for you. Where were you all night?"

"I told you I would be home late."

"Four in the morning is not late in my book. It's beyond just plain late." Eventually there is soft humming, laughter, the sound of the bed thumping against the wall. My parents use sex to soothe all wounds between them. Like bees to orange blossoms, they can never escape each other's nectar.

"God, I love that woman," my father says to me, nodding his head toward my mother. She stands at the sink washing dishes, her hair stringy and damp against her neck. Lately, I am almost repulsed by the things I used to love—the smell of her breath, the softness of her belly, the way she sneezes so incredibly loud that it almost shakes the windows.

"After all these years I just can't get enough of that woman." He says this in a calling-out voice, to make sure she can hear his words over the water in the sink. Then he sings two verses of Tupelo Honey. (She's an angel of the first degree). My mother wiggles her ass in time to the music. This is almost more than I can bear to watch. My father's little asides about how much he loves my mother used to warm my belly and convince me that my world was safe. Now his words feel like grit in my teeth and I no longer want to be a part of their alleged tight little world.

My father, born in the Basque region of Spain, came to this country when he was ten. He always maintained a whisper of an accent. His name is Belasko and he is small and sultry with green eyes. My mother, Dolore, is of Basque ancestry also and grew up in Rhode Island. She and my father met while living on a commune in the mountains of New Hampshire. She is tall, about four inches taller than my father, with a long face and a pear-shaped body. Her hands and feet are exceptionally large. Belasko worked in the apple orchard and Dolore worked in the kitchen, making applesauce, which the commune sold to local markets. It was all a front for the commune's real cash crop—marijuana.

My parents consider themselves gypsies. We move every three years or so, staying just long enough to be recognized in the grocery, at the gas station, long enough to collect a few pieces of furniture. I wonder if anyone notices when we leave. After the commune broke up, they supported themselves as folk musicians, traveling from coffeehouse to coffeehouse, making their way across country, picking up just enough spare change to survive.

They had a theory that a special star was guiding them. That's what happens when you do too many drugs. You get strange notions. They lived in an old converted school bus, covered with my mother's paintings of peace signs and mandalas and, of course, stars.

My father, who was moderately talented, played backup guitar for people like Gordon Lightfoot and Tim Harden and once for Leonard Cohen in Carnegie Hall. Things didn't work out for him in the music industry, yet he doesn't seem to be bitter. His attitude about the whole thing is a shoulder shrug. "Let's just live in the moment," is his pat response to my mother each time she brings it up. He has his photos and a few recordings to prove that he was "almost someone, once." My mother sang back-up harmonies. The two of them did lots of gigs together in the old days, but the music changed and they didn't want to.

They call themselves "original hippies." Sometimes we watch a TV show about the trend in the 60's and early 70's to drop out, turn on and tune in. "Been there, done that," they chirp at the TV. It is all in the past for my parents. When I was born they named me Starry and made an attempt to settle down, which they did as best they could considering their gypsy nature. Now they are middle aged, tired, looking for something they call inner peace. Whatever that is. We move from town to town, state to state, where they pick up small jobs—playing music at coffee houses or clubs, carpentry work, waiting tables, baking pies at local restaurants, giving private music lessons, substitute teaching, driving buses.

Our house is a trailer plopped down in the middle of a field. In the winter it smells like wet clothes and in the summer it smells gritty with dust. We have a dark green couch and a red upholstered rocking chair that makes the house look like it's expecting Christmas at any moment. My father jokingly calls this place Our Mobile Estate. He and my mother like to name each place we have lived in. Our last place was The Quivering Cottage because there were a lot of small earthquakes when we lived there. When I was about three, we rented a Quonset hut that we called Little Snail. My mother's favorite was a bungalow on the edge of a scummy lake. She still calls it The Summer Cottage, as if we were rich people who only vacationed in that insubstantial wooden rattrap. Apartments don't get named. We refer to them by the name of the street they sat on. Walnut with the broken tiles in the kitchen, Cherry with the snake in the bathroom, 5th with the flooded basement. Hallahan Highway had a huge almond tree and Prescott Street came with a flock of parrots in the palm trees.

The two bedrooms in Our Mobile Estate are not much bigger than the beds. My parents have a huge king-size bed with space to shimmy along the wall to get in and out of the room. They have a zebra-striped bedspread and bright yellow sheets. My room is not much bigger than my single mattress on the floor and an old oak dresser full of dings and scratches. We all hate this house. In the winter the cold winds find their way through every chink and crack in the old trailer. When it rains, the metal roof sounds like a musical instrument. That's our favorite thing about this place.

Our most precious belongings have become my parents' records and stereo equipment, my mother's paintings, my father's guitars and his tools. Everything else is replaceable, thanks to second-hand shops. My parents live their lives with their hearts and hands open. "It comes when it comes" is their motto. We seem to make do, as far as I can tell.

The days are long and hot. My best and only friend is Lola, who is tiny and blond, and I believe she is the most beautiful person in the world. Her hands are small and soft and she wears tortoise shell clips in her hair. I compare myself with her and find myself gangly and gawky and really homely. My hair sticks out all over my head, and the best I can do is pull it back with a rubber band to keep it under control.

Lola lives in a compound down at the end of the road—rusty trailers and shacks—with lots of little ones running around the place. Little sisters and brothers, little cousins, little nieces and nephews. My parents call them white trash. White Trash. To me it sounds exotic. Anything that has to do with Lola is exotic to me. She polishes her nails and her big sister puts rollers in Lola's hair when she washes it. Sometimes she lets me pull the rollers out. They slide across her smooth pale hair, making a silken noise, leaving her with a head full of glossy sausage-like ringlets.

Lola's family lives like hillbillies. Her father and uncles grow marijuana in some hidden field back in the mountains. They work hard all summer tending their crop, but after the fall harvest they spend the winter lying around, selling nickel bags to locals and kilos to guys who drive up from L.A. They refer to themselves as farmers and then snicker and giggle about it. Everyone knows how they make their money and no one cares. My parents occasionally buy a baggie full of skunky smelling buds from them. They try to keep this a secret from me.

I'm not nearly as innocent as they seem to think I am. I have my secrets. I commit crimes of my own. Having no talent for music and a voice that sounds like a scratched record, I have my own special talent. Stealing. I started out when I was about three years old taking money out of my father's change jar. I stole dimes (they were my favorite) and stuck them under my mattress. If my parents knew, they never said anything. Maybe they thought it was cute. Then I graduated to pilfering from neighbors: flowers from their gardens, shoes they left by the back door, books they left out on a table. Once I stole a little suitcase that someone forgot to bring into the house when they came to visit the Fogels, our next-door neighbors in Bakersfield. No one ever suspected me. Starry? No, she's a good kid. She wouldn't do anything like that! After sneaking the suitcase behind a shed, I opened it and found nothing but a bunch of pill bottles and Pond's cold cream and sanitary napkins and two shower caps and some shoulder pads. There was a cloth bag full of rollers and hairpins. A bottle of Breck shampoo, some nose drops. I don't know what I expected to find.

Sometimes Lola and I hitch a ride into town with her cousin Lester. Lola lets me sit next to him. He has tattoos and flaming red hair. His hands are freckled with blond hairs springing out of them. I feel funny when I am around Lester. It's a feeling that is new for me. All I have to do is think about Lester and something clenches in my vagina. Sometimes I think about Lester just as I am falling asleep, and then I notice that my hands are between my legs. I don't understand, but just add it to the list of a whole lot of things I don't know. Lola says I'm in love with him. I don't know if that's true. When he looks at me my whole body feels like it's on fire. If that's what being in love is, I want nothing to do with it.

There are a few stores in town, including the Suds and Spuds Laundromat, where you can buy greasy french fries while waiting for your clothes to dry. My best place to shoplift is TG&Y. The saleswomen get to talking and don't pay attention to what you're doing. You could get stark naked and they would still be chatting away and not even notice you. I started with small things—a tiny plastic baby doll, a spool of thread, a package of cough drops, bottles of pink nail polish, which I usually give to Lola as a gift. It was so easy that I moved up to bigger items. Once I stole a box of stationery. Another time, it was a package of panties—white and lacey. We gave them to Lola's older sister for her birthday. They were a big size, but she's pretty fat, so she liked them. By the middle of the summer I am brazen and think of myself as a famous criminal. Last week I stuck a pair of fake pearl earrings in my pocket. I figure in about three years, if I don't lose them, I can give them to my mom for Christmas or something. By then, I'll probably have a job and can tell her I bought them with my own money.

Over the years, I have amassed quite a few things I've snitched, except for the stuff I gave away. I can only steal things that will fit inside a shoebox, so everything I steal has to be pretty small. At some point I might have to graduate to two shoeboxes, but for now, I am able to cram it all in. When I was younger I would hide somewhere and look at all the things in the box about once a week. Now I only glance through the stuff when I have something to add to the collection. A blue glass necklace, a post card stolen from someone's mailbox with a picture of palm trees ("Daniel, Too bad you're not here. Having fun, but miss you. Don't forget to feed the fish. Call the plumber if the toilet gets weird. Love, Bruce"), a tiny pale blue Holy Bible, a cigar with a gold paper ring around it, a pink shell, a pair of men's boxer shorts with walruses, a pair of bright green sunglasses, a paper back book entitled "How to Do Everything Wrong," a gray three-inch ceramic whale, a fountain pen with turquoise ink (dried-out long ago), a Cheerleader Barbie with paper pompoms, a heart-shaped mirror.

The first time I see my dad with that other woman, Lola and I had hitched a ride into town with Lester to do some minor shoplifting. We are walking past The Joint. The Joint is a bar behind the auto supply store. My parents do gigs there once in a while and sometimes we all drive down there for dinner. They make great coleslaw and really greasy onion rings. Lola and I like to explore, to walk down alleys and search out something—anything that might prove interesting.

This particular day we're scuffling through the gravel behind some of the stores when I think I see my dad's station wagon parked next to a delivery truck, kind of hidden. Lola notices it too.

"Hey, Starry, ain't that your dad's car?" Something in my stomach does not feel right. Why is his car parked that way? He told my mom he was driving over to Fresno to do some carpentry work. I shush her and start to walk away. "Where you goin' Starry? Isn't that him? See, isn't that him sittin' in the car?" I don't want to look, but Lola grabs my arm and pulls me behind the delivery truck so we can get a better look. Sure enough, it is my father. With a woman. I have no idea who she is. I can't imagine (don't want to imagine) what he is doing here with her. My father, who is constantly telling me how much he adores my mother, hanging out with another woman? I start to tell myself that maybe they're talking about business. Then Lola pokes me really hard in the ribs. "Lookit," she hisses in my ear. My ear is wet from her spray of saliva.

"No," I tell her. "I don't want to look. Let's just go, Lola." I try to pull away but she has a death hold on my entire left arm and I can't budge. I follow the trail of her eyes, still afraid to see what she's staring at yet knowing that I have to be brave and look.

Through the rear window of my father's dark blue Ford station wagon, I see the back of a woman's head. She is blond and her hair is kind of frizzy. Definitely bleached. My father's arm is around her and he is facing her and I can see his mouth moving. Every few seconds he leans close to her and kisses her. Then I see his hand behind her head, stirring up her frizzy hair, messing it up even worse than it already is. Then he kisses her for a long time.

I start to feel nauseated, like I ate something bad. I am having a hard time breathing and turn around, bend over and retch. Lola is so busy watching my father that she doesn't even seem to notice.

"Hot damn. What a show. Just wait till your mom finds out. He'll be singin' Tupelo Honey to her till the cows come home." Lola's laugh is high and wheezy and I have to kick her to get her to shut up. I need to run to escape something horrible that I'm feeling. I have to get as far away as I can.

For days I walk around feeling like I've been slapped across the face. It's like the time I woke up in the middle of the night to find my father's hand under my pillow replacing my tooth with a quarter. This is worse. That was about the tooth fairy, but this is about the whole issue of lying, not to mention possible divorce. My parents give me very few rules, except for lying. I know that if they ever ask me if I'm stealing, I would have to tell them the truth. In their eyes, stealing is a bad choice, but lying is a fatal flaw. Every time the phone rings, I worry that it's one of those old ladies at TG&Y calling to tell them about my shoplifting.

Now, I suppose I should also worry that each time the phone rings it will be that blonde bimbo calling to let us know that Belasko is leaving us for her. I always believed everything my parents told me. No matter what it was. Now I mistrust everything that comes out of their mouths.

"We're having mac and cheese for dinner tonight," my father calls in from the kitchen.

"Really? Are you sure?"

"What do you mean. Of course I'm sure. Why?"

"I don't know, Dad. Just want to make sure."

"Your mom's working late tonight at the restaurant. She won't be home till you're already in bed."

"She's working?"

"That's what I said. Working."

"You sure, Dad? You sure she's working?"

"Yeah, up at the burger joint."

"Really?"

"Starry, what's with you? Yes, I'm sure. What's your problem?"

"Nothing. I don't have a problem." Then I hear my father mumble something under his breath—something about something about adolescence. I feel triumphant for some reason, suddenly older than I was just a few days ago.

Lola and I are inseparable and most summer nights she sleeps in my bed with me. She loves the peacefulness in my house—just the two of us and my parents. She and I sleep like spoons in a drawer. I love the feel of her round stomach against my backside. We sleep in thin cotton baby doll pajamas, our legs brushing against each other. Lola is already shaving so her legs are prickly. The open window lets in hot dust and pollen that cover the oak dresser with a golden film. In the morning we write our names in the powder and make polka dots with our fingertips. Lola wheezes when she sleeps—a soft gentle whining in her lungs, so close that her moist breath dampens my neck.

Lola is glad to get away from her house and all the commotion. White Trash noise is what we call it—gunning motors, laughing, beer bottles thrown into metal cans, babies crying, twangy music on the radio. She says it's never quiet at her place. Not ever. My parents work strange hours, sometimes late at night playing music at a local bar or waiting tables. Lola and I listen to records—Bob Dylan, the Grateful Dead, Cat Stevens, the Beatles, steady beat and lyrics worth listening to. We know all the words and hold hairbrush microphones to our mouths, pretending we're up there on stage. Bright lights and cheering crowds. The house smells of incense and hot sand. My mother hangs huge pots of pothos and grape ivy in the corners. She claims it helps us breath better. She tried making an herb garden behind the house, but between the dry heat and her tendency to neglect everything, all the plants died.

Ever since Lola and I caught my father with another woman, she has been bothering me about it. I try so hard to pretend I didn't see what I saw, sometimes almost convincing myself it was a bad dream, until Lola opens her big mouth and has to bring it up.

"Your dad's got a girlfriend, your dad's got a girlfriend." She is singing this, like it's something on the hit parade. I tell her to shut up. She sings it again. I tell her it's not true. "Yes it is, we seen him."

"It's not his girlfriend. He's married. He can't have a girlfriend."

"Whadaya mean? Of course he can have a girlfriend. All married guys have girlfriends. My dad had one and he run away with her."

"Well, my dad's not going to do that. He loves my mom. He just wouldn't do that." Even as I speak these words, I hear how naïve I sound.

"Oh yeah? And how do you know?"

"Because he loves my mom. They do it almost every night. I can hear them." The truth is, they haven't been doing it as often. I don't even want to think about what that means.

"Starry, it's a good thing you got me as a friend. Bein' as how I'm eighteen months older, I know stuff you have no idea about." She is always reminding me she is older (actually only fourteen months older, but I have given up pointing out that minor detail). "You know what? Doin' it don't mean a thing. Men gotta do it all the time and that's why they all got girlfriends on the side."

"Not my dad. Maybe he was kissing that frizzy-head bitch, but there's got to be a good reason."

"Yeah. Cause he's doin' her."

"Shut up, Lola. You don't know. I think maybe he felt sorry for her 'cause of her hair and all. Maybe she's really ugly and he feels bad for her and wants her to feel good. My dad's like that. It was probably a mercy kiss. It doesn't mean anything." I am trying so hard to convince myself that Lola just shrugs her shoulders, shakes her head, rolls her eyes and starts whistling.

Cousin Lester drives us into town a few weeks later. If he knows about our secret pilfering, he never says a word. Lola and I head to our favorite place to do our business, the TG&Y. We skip down the aisles, thinking it makes us seem younger and less suspicious. My dad's birthday is coming up and I am looking at a rack of the only things in the store that might be appropriate for a man. Barbeque forks, skewers, chef's hats, long matches, bags of charcoal, oven mitts... Unfortunately, we are vegetarians at home, so I move down the aisle toward the flash lights and batteries and other possibilities. I am trying to figure out how I can sneak a clock radio out of the store without being caught and what story I can tell him about how I paid for it. Out of the corner of my eye I see Lola skipping toward me very fast. Keeping in character with the we're-younger-than-we-really-are disguise, she looks totally ridiculous and I start to laugh. Really loud. I can't help myself.

When Lola reaches me, she clamps her hand across my mouth, tells me with her eyes to shut up and pulls me down until we are crouching and walking to the end of the aisle.

"Look," she hisses at me.

"Where" I hiss back at her.

"Right there, stupid." She points her finger, keeping her hand very close to her chest. "Over by the make-up department."

The first thing I notice is that three women are grouped together, talking to each other. Then I see it. That same blond frizzy hair. They are each wearing the red employees smock with the plastic name tag pinned over the left tittie.

"Damn, it's her."

"Yup, it is. The one your dad's doin' it with. Right here." I feel sick, like I'm running a fever. Lola puts her arm around me and we crouch-walk back down the aisle. On the way I grab a yellow flashlight and stick it in my pocket. Fuck TG&Y. Now we'll have to find somewhere else to do our dirty work.

My mind is racing with crazy thoughts. Does this woman with the frizzy hair know I am Belasko's daughter? Don't I look just like him? Is she spying on me for him? What if she mentions that she saw a thirteen-year-old skipping around the store impersonating a six-year-old that, oh by the way, looks a lot like you, Belasko. Maybe she calls him honey or sweetheart. Maybe he calls her those things.

"Damn. Do you think we'll have to find another place to shoplift? Do you think that bitch knows your dad has a daughter? Maybe he showed her your picture, Starry. Maybe she'll recognize you." I can't answer one of these questions. I am feeling dizzy and have to sit down on a bench in front of the barber shop. I take the yellow flashlight out of my pocket and throw it into the street, where a huge cement truck flattens it with a cracking sound.

I keep waiting for my dad to say something to me about this, but he seems to be oblivious to anything that I do. I am still looking for a sign that something about him is different at home, but he continues to sing stupid songs to my mother and me. He still tries to get me to learn to play his guitar, since it's obvious I have not one bit of talent in the singing department. Belasko is Belasko, never changing. For that matter, my mother is her usual distant self, like she's there but not really. She just smokes and reads a lot this summer.

I am just about to fall asleep, feeling myself drift away, imagining I am lying on a rubber raft in the middle of a pool. It's my favorite sensation these days, dissolving into the sweet darkness of sleep. I hear a loud engine roaring to a stop, like it's coming through a tunnel and I wonder if I am beginning to dream. There is pounding at the front door. It continues for a while until I realize it's not a dream, but that someone is out there banging. I wait to see if my father will answer the door and it seems to take forever, but I finally hear him come out of his bedroom.

"Who is it?" There's no answer, so my father asks the same question, only this time much much louder. "Who the hell is it? I'm not opening the fucking door until you tell me who you are." My bedroom window faces the front of the trailer, so I can peek out to see who's on the porch. Who I see is a guy in a wheelchair. I'm not sure, but it looks like he has no legs. I've never seen anyone without any legs and I feel my insides start to shake.

"Open the door, you asshole. You should know who I am." I wait. I listen. My father is silent for a long time. By now my mother is out of bed and I can hear her hissing something in his ear about a gun. "Take the gun, dammit. He's probably got one." She has the gun in her hand and forces him to take it.

Belasko's voice is calm now, and his words come out slow and loud. "Tell me who you are and I'll open the door. Just tell me who you are."

"Does the name Sheryl Lynn mean anything to you, man?" I hear my father swear under his breath and then he opens the door.

By now I am able to sneak into the front room and hide behind the red chair. Belasko is in his boxers and my mother's in a short terrycloth robe, standing behind him. I watch as my father slowly unlatches the door and opens it. He has a gun in his hand, but he keeps it behind his back. Out on the porch is a legless man in a wheelchair. Apparently, he was able to pull himself up the steps. He has huge arms and is shiny with sweat. "Like I said, man, does the name Sheryl Lynn mean anything to you?"

"Shit man," my father replies. He just stands there staring at the legless guy, staring at his non-existent legs, shaking his head. "I had no idea. She never told me about you. You her husband or something?"

"Who the fuck you think I am? Her hair dresser? Her gardener? Her shrink? Asshole." My father just stands there, shaking his head back and forth, his shoulders slumped almost like a cartoon character. He pulls the gun out from behind his back and lays it on the table.

"Hey, I don't want any trouble. She never told me anything about you. I got my wife and kid here." The legless man stares at the gun on the table. His hand is twitching to reach out and grab it. I can tell. I can feel his wanting to. He is wearing a black sleeveless shirt that says Vietnam Vet. You Gotta Problem with That? His jaw pulses, like he's squeezing his teeth together.

"I served in Nam, man. I lost my legs for my country, man. What'd you ever do for your country? You're not even a fuckin' citizen, Mister. She told me. She told me everything and I didn't even have to beat it out of her. She told me every little thing." He says those words slowly. With that he starts pounding the wall beside him. He pounds over and over and over until there is a hole in the phony paneling and his fist is bloody and pulpy. My parents just stand there and watch. Dolore shrugs her shoulders, finally walks into the bedroom and slams the door shut. The legless man can see me hiding behind the chair. My father has no idea I am there watching.

"Hey. It's enough. You broke my wall. I got the message, man. I won't go near her. Just get the hell out of here." The legless man just sits there staring at my father for a long time. His face isn't angry or scared or sad or anything. He has no expression at all. He looks almost like a statue, except his chest is moving up and down a lot and his breathing is loud. This goes on for a long time, long enough for me to wonder exactly where his legs are and how much of them is left on his body. My father finally takes his wheelchair and pulls it backwards down the steps and pushes him out to the road where his car is. He opens the car door for him, helps him into the driver's seat then folds the guy's chair and throws it in the back seat. They talk for a few minutes and then Belasko comes back into the house. When he sees me standing by the front door he yells at me to get back to bed.

My heart is pounding too much for me to go back to sleep. I turn and turn in my bed a million times. I can hear my father coughing his marijuana cough and smell it coming from their bedroom. Their voices are loud. They must think I'm asleep.

"I should have known. What made me think you would keep your promise? Goddamn, you stinking liar. I can't take this any more. Just get the hell out already."

"Oh, Babe. It was really nothing. You know I can't help myself. I'm sorry, sweetheart. You're right, I am an asshole, a jerk, a liar, a creep, a major fuck-up, a pervert, an adulterer, a cheater, a schemer, a user, an abuser, a maggot."

My mother continues, as if the sentence had never ended. "A weakling, a child, a baby, a prick, an ass kisser, a sick fuck, a disappointment to the world, a lousy singer and a lousy lay. If you can't control yourself, Belasko, just get the hell out of my life. I am sick of this shit. Grow up already."

This goes on for a long time. Someone keeps leaving the bedroom to go into the kitchen to get a beer, to run water in the sink, to lock and unlock the front door, to turn the porch light off and on. By now, I am once again drifting off into the darkness of sleep. My parents, voices sound a million miles away. By the morning, everything is normal, except for the hole in the wall. My father is snoring on the couch, but this is nothing new.

We never talk about it. It's like it never happened and sometimes I can almost convince myself that it was a bad dream. Except for the bloody hole in the wall.

About a quarter mile across the fields is the local commuter airport. There are two flights daily to and from L.A. and others from Fresno, Stockton, Bakersfield, San Jose, Sacramento and Oakland. Recently the runway was enlarged to accommodate jets. At this point we have one jet daily, originating in San Jose and taking off at 8:00 pm for Los Angeles. Each night we can hear the incredible roaring noise, louder than anything I have ever heard in my life. Our road is at the end of the long airstrip, running in the same direction, which makes it seem like a continuation of the runway. Each jet seems to skim the top of the houses, barely missing us, until it turns and twists off to the south. My mother worries that one day a plane will lose control and crash into our living room. My father strokes her hair and lights up the water pipe for her each time she says this. "Have a smoke, Baby. It'll calm you down. There's nothing to worry about. Those pilots know what they're doing."

All summer long, Lola and I have been attempting to get sucked up into the updraft, not realizing that this would mean ultimate death. We had stopped reading the book on jet propulsion just before it got to that point. It was way overdue at the school library. Something about this whole process is addictive and I anticipate it all day. The thought of it stays in the back of my mind, like a storm brewing, slowly filling the horizon of each day with a strange glow. As the sun slides lower and lower in the sky, I feel something rising in my body—a kind of heat that begins at the bottom of my spine and slowly creeps farther and farther up until it lodges itself in my chest and across my shoulder blades. There is something almost robotic about how my body reacts, as if I have no control over myself.

As Lola and I stand at the edge of the field, we hear the roaring of the jet engines. That sound grows and expands in the evening air and Lola's eyes get bigger and bigger until they seem to engulf her entire face with their blueness. We listen to the whooshing noise and then on the horizon emerges a huge silver bird, barreling toward us. I can reach out my hand and almost feel the hot steel nose of the plane. As it gets closer, it lifts slowly, almost painfully off the ground. "OK. Now!" we yell in unison. Then starts the long run, our legs taking us down the middle of the semi-paved road, the plane approaching us from behind. I can feel it, the enormous energy of the jets sucking in air, pollen, dust, brush, insects, my own breath. I feel like I am about to fly.

"Lift me. Lift me," I scream at the top of my lungs. I can't hear anything but the roar of the huge engines, but I know that Lola is screaming the same words. "Lift me, Lift me!" With our arms spread-eagle we run to the end of the road and across the field, the wind whipping our hair, sucking us upward and upward. Lift me! Take me away! My heart sings, my heart pleads. Pull me up and over this dismal place. This monotonous land. This stifling life. I want to move across the sky, invisible, over this pale dry dessert, this gray brush, the ramshackle houses, the small lives below. Lift me into the depths of heaven, where the sky is clear and deep blue and the air is cold in my chest. As I run, my heart racing and my legs pumping, the sweat trails down my neck, pooling inside my belly button, across the small of my back, sliding down into the crack of my buttocks. I can feel the heat rising, liquid light surging up my spine. Like a fire. Like an electrical charge. My head sizzles. My nose runs as I suck in exhaust fumes until I am dizzy.

I continue to run after the plane passes overhead, enters my field of vision and disappears into the darkening sky. I run until my legs begin to tremble and I have to let my body come to a slow stop. Lola and I both flop on the ground. She laughs and gasps for air. She doesn't notice that I never laugh with her any more. I have understood for a while now that what started as a game for each of us has ceased to become a game for me. My lungs ache and my heart is pounding in my ears. It is the sound of breaking disappointment. I have been left on this ground, still in this life. For me, it's another shattered attempt to escape. This is something I can never explain to her. Above us a ribbon of dark smoke marks the path of the jet, and the sky turns indigo with streaks of pink and orange.

"Did you feel it? It was strong today, wasn't it? I swear my feet left the ground." Lola laughs while she talks. I agree, trying to convince her, or even myself, that this is all just some stupid fun.

"Maybe next time."

"Yeah, maybe tomorrow." By now it is almost dark. I walk across the field, through the dry brush, sidestepping the small tumbleweeds of summer. I keep my eyes on the ground, not wanting to look up into the sky, not wanting to look ahead at the cluster of ugly rundown trailers and shacks. I go back into the house where the heat has been collecting all day. My mother, who has been reading <u>War and Peace</u> all summer, looks up from her book and smiles at me. There are three fans blowing the blistering air around.

"You look hot, Starry. Why don't you take a shower and I'll make us some dinner. Your dad called and he'll be home soon." She pulls her long hair behind her ears, lights another cigarette, and makes a shooing motion with her hands, indicating she wants to continue reading for a while. My mother sneezes. The windows rattle. God, I hate this fucking life.

In the shower I smell my sweat in the steamy air. It is astringent, like an animal smell. My mother has the same odor. I know this means I am growing up, that soon I'll be bleeding, like Lola and her older sisters. I soap my hands, make fists and scrub my armpits. As I cup the roundness of my titties, I can feel their growing heaviness. Lola thinks I have good tits. She says the nipples are dark as molasses and I guess that's a good thing. I soap my legs and inspect the fine dark hairs along my shinbone.

I scrub my head, squinting to keep the shampoo out of my eyes. I can smell onions frying with garlic and saffron. My dad should be home by now, his hair tied back in a ponytail. He'll drink a Coors.

I know that Lola will show up wearing her baby dolls under a huge sweatshirt and that she'll eat some saffron rice with us, even though she's already had dinner. I know that we'll stay up late talking about her cousin Lester. She will cuddle up behind me when I turn off the light and breathe behind my ear as we listen to my parents murmur and giggle in the next room. Or bicker. I know that soon my parents and I will move, that I'll never see Lola again. I wonder if she will miss me, if whenever she thinks of me, she will also think of my father in his car behind the bar. Maybe she'll forget about it. Maybe I will. I feel in my chest that I could easily start to cry. I have never felt this way about leaving a place, never had anyone I thought I might miss. I scrub my head even harder until it feels sore and I forget about missing Lola, about my father, about the lady with the blonde frizzy hair.

With the water hitting me like hot needles I wonder if I will ever be able to fly away. It suddenly occurs to me that perhaps my attempts to be lifted into the updraft of the daily jet to L.A. is nothing more than a childhood fantasy. I feel like a veil has been lifted and my vision is gradually becoming clearer and clearer, as if a glowing light has suddenly illuminated a place within me which has been, up until this very moment, dark and murky. It reminds me of the time I realized that the packages under the Christmas tree were things my parents had bought, not gifts delivered by Santa. Resigned and somehow relieved.

I am standing naked in front of the full-length mirror in my room. Outside, the sky is the color of a blue velvet dress. My round face is still flushed from running, my arms and legs brown from the sun. I have very big feet. My dad says it's a sign that I'll be a "big girl" like my mom. He claims he likes big girls. I try to remember if that frizzy head with the legless husband is a big girl too. My stomach and midriff and breasts look as pale as a bowl of cream. My legs are getting longer and my knees look like tulip bulbs, full of lumps. Silky hair is starting to grow between my legs and it feels like tiny feathers.

I barely recognize this person I face in the mirror and imagine that in another three years I won't even remember the person I am now. I'll be living in another house, in another back-water town, still listening to my parents bicker and hum on the other side of the wall. Sadness hangs like a mist inside my chest, under my ribs, close to where my heart is. A place now dark and threatening, like the reverberation of thunder way off in the distance.

"Lift me. Lift me." I whisper to my reflection in the mirror. My eyes are dark pools filled with longing. I can hear Lola knocking on the screen door. I can hear my parents banging plates in the kitchen. I can feel my own heart beating just under my breastbone as I slip into my baby dolls.

Epilogue

My father's three families showed up for his funeral. Hye Su, the woman he was with before my mother, came with her son (my half brother) Arlen. This was the first time I had ever met them. I had, in fact, lived my life believing I was his only child. Arlen, with his vaguely familiar Korean face, ignored me. Hye Su came up to me and my mother and bowed her head. We needed no words. My father had left Hye Su and their son when Arlen was a toddler.

There was something soft and wispy about Doreen, the woman who had sent us the invitation. So unlike my mother, she wore filmy flowing layers of fabric and had wrapped herself in a thin black shawl. She tried to be gracious, inviting us all back to her house for a "bite to eat". Hye Su pretended not to hear her, and my mother bowed out, not so gracefully, announcing that she was a strict vegetarian and ate only organic food. The funeral, held in Fresno, was small.

It wasn't until my father's death that pieces of the puzzle of my childhood moved into place, showing me a more complete image. I have a small collection of photos that tell a partial tale, or at least a tale that I had been telling myself was the story of my early life. My parents lost or misplaced every camera they ever owned. From my entire childhood, there are probably 25 photographs that have by now faded, giving each image an orange, almost disembodied flush.

We could have been any family of our ilk living in the 60's, 70's and 80's, my mother wearing long tie-dyed dresses, my father with a pony tail and striped bellbottoms, me with a pacifier in my mouth in a droopy diaper, another one of me dressed up as a popsicle for Halloween. My mother and me, in front of a series of pathetic looking Christmas trees, wearing the attire of the times (leather vests, high white boots, ponchos with fringes hanging almost to the floor, mini skirts with high heels), my father and one of the many dogs that got loose and ran away and were never seen again. My parents and a few of their friends from the commune in New Hampshire. In the process of moving every few years, most of my school pictures were lost, except for my fourth grade class picture. In the crowd I look non-descript, like any nine-year old, my hair in a sloppy pony tail, a lopsided-smile, standing pigeon toed like half the girls in my class.

My parents did manage to save a few snapshots of them on stage with somewhat well-known bands. My father leaning back, his leg bent as if walking up a step, fingering his guitar as he looks down toward the strings, his dark hair wild and wet like a halo around his head. My mother stands off to the side singing into a microphone, her mouth open, eyes closed, hands covering her ears.

I hadn't seen or heard from my father since the day he walked out on my mother and me over fifteen years before. According to Doreen, his death was sudden and unexpected. He died at 63 of complications of viral pneumonia.

After the funeral my mother and I stood over my father's grave. She looked especially tired that afternoon. Perhaps from the drive in from Marin County, perhaps from actual sadness about my father's death, although that seemed unlikely. Visibly aged, her face told the story of a roller coaster kind of life. Great highs and great lows. Her hair, which had always been wispy and mousy, was now even more so. Her eyes seemed sunken, with dark rings around them. She wore a loose blue skirt and a deep red blouse that seemed too big for her, giving her a strange almost patriotic look.

Dolore used to be curvy, but now it seemed that all her curves had given in to gravity and were hiding somewhere around her hidden ankles. She had always been a fortress to me. Huge and solid as a cathedral. Whatever sentiment she was feeling stays locked inside and nothing, not even her eyes, revealed any emotional ripple in her being. I watched my mother light a cigarette, take a deep draw and flick the hot ash into the freshly dug earth on the top of my father's casket. I remembered how my father, who was troubled by bronchial problems, tried to get her to quit.

Later, as we ate lunch at a local Denny's (a restaurant totally void of anything even resembling organic) my mother asked me if I had ever noticed that there were no pictures of her and my father's wedding.

"I never thought about it. I just figured you lost them in all the moves."

"There never were any pictures. We never got married."

"You and Dad were never married? Why didn't you tell me?"

"Weren't we weird enough? We didn't want to add any more reasons for you to be embarrassed by us. Besides, it was no one's business. I didn't need to be married with him. Lots of people live together and have children and never get married. We both knew it was just a stupid legal formality. We were hippies, you know. Formality was bullshit."

Dolore's eyes slid my way. I saw what I might look like in another 30 years and it was not a reassuring thought. She held her tuna fish sandwich up to her mouth and took a huge bite. Her eyes never left my face and I knew enough to ask no more questions. Between bites of her sandwich, sips of her coffee and nibbles of potato chips, she talked. She told me things I never knew, mostly about my father, filling in the blanks and answering questions I didn't know I had wanted answered. She spread before me a quilt of facts and truths and probably some untruths. From the time I was mature enough to be curious about my parents, I had always had a feeling that they had a secret. Our lifestyle was unpredictable, uncertain and filled with geographical upheavals. No one ever explained those immediate pack-up-everything-and-leave-in-the-middle-of-the-night events that occurred every few years.

What I didn't know was that my father was running away from

his past. Besides trying to escape his support payments to Hye Su for his son, my mother admitted to me that he was running from some minor scrapes with the law. Stupid stuff like unpaid traffic fines, political gatherings, refusing to pay his taxes. According to her, all minor stuff. She didn't say it, but I figured there was something about selling or dealing drugs in my father's past. And maybe a little thievery, I thought to myself.

"Starry, that man could be a stubborn son-of-a-bitch. I just kept quiet about everything. Each time it seemed like we had settled somewhere, he would have a dream or some kind of crazy intuition. Then he was frantic and we had to get the hell out of wherever we were living and find a new place." I thought about the man with no legs showing up in the middle of the night. I realized that it was only a few weeks after that event that my parents announced our next departure. "Other than his addiction to other women, Belasko was good to me. I have no complaints. And by the time he left me, I didn't need him. He still wanted to fuck and I was tired and just wanted my solitude. I wished him luck. He sent money for us when he could. That's all I really wanted from him."

I asked my mother if she thought my father had loved me. I knew it was a strange question to ask, but I was never quite sure how he felt about me, and his sudden taking-off left me with so much self-doubt and even a little self-blame. Even though he never failed to send birthday and Christmas cards stuffed with cash, I never connected those acts with feelings of love. I assumed it was guilt that was at play. My mother shrugged her shoulders and wiped her mouth with her napkin.

"Starry, there's something you ought to know about your father. He loved whatever and whoever was in front of him. End of story." I saw bitterness and resignation in her dark eyes. Then she lit a cigarette and used her dinner plate as an ashtray as she looked past me, out the window and into the hot parking lot. I could see the annoyed waitress rushing towards us to remind my mother that this was a non-smoking restaurant.

My flight home was delayed three hours because of a tornado south of Chicago. I was feeling drained, anxious and frustrated. My father's funeral still seemed like a dream and saying goodbye to my mother was difficult. By the time I was seated on the plane, the atmosphere was tense. Passengers were cranky, hungry, pissed off. Two rows ahead of me a small girl cried, as her bewildered father tried to mollify her. He called her Pumpkin. He sang a nursery rhyme to her. He tried to show her the pictures in a magazine. Nothing seemed to soothe this child. I watched the father slowly, by degrees, become unraveled. As the plane took off, he pointed out the window, talking into her ear. She wanted to crawl on his lap and he kept pointing to the Fasten Seatbelt sign, trying to explain what it meant. In my fascination with their interactions, I had barely noticed that the plane was already in the air. Miraculously, it had lifted without the help of my clutching the armrests and my silent prayer.

Eventually the child settled down and I closed my eyes, hoping to doze. For some reason, the interaction between the man and his daughter stuck with me. I wondered how my father would have handled the same situation. My mind drifted in and out of memories of Belasko—his beautiful voice, his silly singing to my mother, the way he focused on his guitar when he played. I remembered the afternoon I graduated from high school. After the ceremony, the three of us went out for Italian food and then we dropped Dolore off at home. My father said he had something special he wanted to share with me. We drove through golden fields, across the flat valley behind Salinas and up toward the foothills. He pulled off on a rutted road that led to a stand of live oak trees and parked. I had no idea what he was doing.

My father reached behind his seat and pulled out his guitar. For a long time he simply plucked the strings, looking out at the trees. I remembered that he was wearing a wrinkled white buttoned-down shirt—one of the only times I ever saw him make an attempt to look somewhat formal.

"Dad, why did you bring me here?" I wanted to be with my friends, celebrating and drinking beer.

"You know, you kind of look like your mom did when I first met

her. *If she had been more beautiful, I mean. You are very pretty, Starry. You make me proud.*" He continued to noodle around with the guitar and as the chords seemed to organize themselves, I could hear a kind of melody emerge. Then his voice, his wonderful tenor voice sang the words to a song I had not heard before. I never forgot those words and for years I thought it was something he had written until I heard that same song on a TV show called *Blasts from the Past*. The song is named "Pack Up Your Sorrows" and was written by Richard Farina. "*If somehow you could pack up your sorrows, give them all to me. You would lose them, I know how to use them, give them all to me.*"

Under the shade of those old trees with their twisted arms above us, I watched my father's eyes glaze with tears, and when the song was done, he turned his head away from me. "*One time your mom and I spent the night under trees just like this. We spread an old quilt and watched the owls and bats fly around. We talked all night. That's what it's like when you're in the beginning of a relationship, you know. We're pretty sure it's the night you were conceived. It was a starry night and we decided that if we ever had a daughter, we would name her Starry. We were tired of being a duet and decided it was time to become a trio. You made us that trio, Starry.*"

"Let me remind you, Dad. I'm tone deaf."

"Yeah, I've noticed that. It's okay. We're still a trio, honey."

"What would you have named me if I were a boy?" He took a breath, squinted and turned his head to face me.

"We didn't really talk about it. We just knew you were a girl. I guess we would have named a boy something like Cosmo or Mercury. I sang your mother this song. It was romantic. She always has sadness, that woman. My singing used to make her smile." He went into his pocket and pulled out a stick of peppermint gum and offered it to me. For a long time he simply sat and stared off into the middle distance. I wanted to reach out and touch my father, but it seemed too contrived, like in a sad movie. Instead, I looked at the pale sky and counted the seconds. We drove home in silence. He left us a year later, to the day.

If Belasko really did take my mother's sorrows, I am not sure. It seems that he might have taken some and replaced them with some *others. For the most part, I believe that our sorrows refine us, in the way a tiny paintbrush completes a portrait by filling in the fine lines of character. As a child, I imagined my family as a tight circle, and after my father left us I still imagined his presence with us, holding each of our hands as we circled through this life. But now that he is truly gone, there seems to be a void. I have an empty hand with no one to hold onto it. My mother and I will have to learn to hold onto each other now, without the invisible Belasko as a conduit.*

Cynthia

Cynthia is in a corner of the play yard. Crouched, hidden in the shadows of a huge tree, next to a crude rabbit hutch. She cries quietly as she watches the large brown rabbit munch on tough green curls of kale. She is four years old, small for her age, with huge black eyes.

I approach her quietly and ask "Que paso? Que paso, Cynthia?" The small child has no answer, and I sit down in the dirt next to her. I am a pre-school teacher and Cynthia is in my class. There is something about this child that touches my heart. Lately, she has been very emotional, difficult to deal with. She will scream and cry when asked to do something she doesn't want to do, like clean up or lie down during naptime. Most days I spend naptime holding her in my arms and rocking her until she is relaxed enough to lie on her mat.

"Tell me, Cynthia. Que paso?" She shakes her head no and continues to cry softly as she sucks her two middle fingers. Her nails are dirty from playing in the dirt. She is barely aware of me sitting beside her.

I imagine what is going on in her mind, in her tiny body. I know the story about her family—about the abusive older brother and the things he has done to Cynthia and her sister. I had already heard about last night—the police had been called (no one seems to know who placed the call), and they came to the house to question the little girls. I imagine Cynthia sitting quietly in the corner, sucking her two middle fingers, refusing to talk. I could see her older sister, Bibiana, talking and talking—telling everything.

"My brother, he touch me here and then down here, and then he hit me too. He always do this to me, my brother." Bibiana, already six, is vivacious and talkative. I imagine their mother, her round Guatemalan face stricken. The police took him to juvenile hall. I imagine Cynthia not being able to hear her sister's words, yet knowing from gestures and the expression on her sister's face what she is telling the police.

Cynthia is my translator. My understanding of the Spanish language is limited and I don't always understand what some of my students are trying to tell me. And many of the students speak very little English, so they don't always understand what I am saying to them. Cynthia is always by my side in these situations, translating my words into Spanish and their words into English. She has a natural ability with languages and I have taught her a few Italian words also.

I pull Cynthia onto my lap and rock her gently. "It's okay, Cynthia. You are safe here." I whisper into her tangled hair. She answers that she wants her mommy. She finds my hands and holds them in front of her face. My nails are round and smooth, and I am wearing two silver rings. There is a bandage on my index finger. Cynthia pulls it off, wanting to see what is underneath it.

"Que paso?" the small child asks.

"I cut it on a piece of broken glass." She touches the scratch with the tips of her fingers. Her fingers are wet and puckered from being sucked, her hands small and brown. She examines my hands—they are wide and strong and smooth, unlike her mother's hands, which are rough from cleaning chemicals and hard work. She takes my hand and places the palm against her chest, holding it as she continues to cry quietly. Her nose is running and she wipes it with the sleeve of her sweater. I can feel Cynthia's heart fluttering under the thin bones of her chest.

A Table to Kill For

The Table

The plan. The plan was to kill him. Somehow. Ruthie was sure she would figure that part out later. Once he's dead, Ruthie thought, I can walk into his house and take whatever I want.

He had this table Ruthie had been coveting ever since she first saw it, the day she knocked on his door to collect for some deserving cause. March of Dimes, Breast Cancer, Jerry's Kids. Ruthie couldn't remember the charity, but she certainly remembered that table.

It sat in the entryway, just left of the front door. Small, painted with maroon and deep orange stripes and flecked with gold leaf, it called to her. Ruthie almost swallowed her gum when she saw it. He gave her a fifty dollar check and started to shut the door.

"Wait" Ruthie said. "That table. It's really unusual."

"Yeah," he said proudly. "I picked it up at the thrift store."

"The thrift store? You're kidding me."

"Yeah. It was sitting under a box of Christmas tree ornaments. I needed something right here by the front door, and this was the perfect size. I went to the library and did some research and found out it was made either in Turkey or Syria. Some place like that." Ruthie took note of the table and saw that he was using it as a catch-all for the newspaper, his keys and an empty coffee cup.

She wanted that table. Ruthie knew it would be perfect in her bedroom. She would keep it clean and uncluttered, never as a place to leave old coffee cups or her keys. She had daydreams about the table, imagining she was in Turkey, sitting next to the man who had fashioned it from the wood of an old apricot tree. Ruthie imagined watching him fit the pieces together and then painting it with a two-inch wide soft bristled brush, carefully creating the striped colors and then brushing on pieces of gold leaf.

"All I have to do is kill the guy, make off with the table and whisk it into my own house. He lives alone, so no one will know he's dead for a while. He obviously has no sentimental attachment to it. He bought it in the thrift store, for Christ's sake." Ruthie uttered these words to herself as she made a grilled cheese sandwich a few nights later. "It's the perfect crime. I just have to figure out how to do it."

Ruthie knew that having a plan was important. Very important. More important than a normal plan like what to cook for dinner or which movie to see. How to kill someone and not get caught— now that was something Ruthie had to consider very carefully.

She watched his house, which was easy considering that he lived just across the street from her. Like a good detective, she took notes. Every other Monday his gardener came. Each morning he was out walking his dog Tiger by 7:00. Then he walked Tiger seven nights a week at 6:00. His maid came every other Thursday around 3:00 in the afternoon and was usually gone by 5:30. He never had visitors and only left the house three or four times a week, usually around noon. And so on and so on.

Colder than a Sow's Tit

Ruthie made a chart of her neighbor's schedule and taped it next to her living room window, where she sat with her binoculars watching his house. Sometimes she was able to see into the front room early in the morning. He always woke up at 6 and routinely sat in a chair by his window with a cup of coffee. He went out for the paper each morning by 6:30 and always took Tiger out for his morning walks at 7:00 sharp. He wore the same red hooded sweatshirt every morning, his aging body partially bent forward, walking slowly.

Several times Ruthie trailed him. He went by the creek and Tiger always deposited a pile close to the huge sycamore tree, where it was left to ferment, steam rising up into the cold morning air.

Meanwhile, life was waiting to happen. As Ruthie spied on her neighbor, she planned what that table would look like next to her bed. Should she paint the walls? A pale coral? Golden yellow? She would of course have to buy a new comforter and sheets. Maybe some fuchsia-colored silk pillows with sequins and bugle beads. Stripes would look good, to match the stripes on the table. She spent hours imagining all the possibilities. "I think I'm obsessed," she whispered to herself.

To kill someone—to murder in cold blood for nothing more than a table—seemed a bit ridiculous to her. The time she had gone to his house to collect his donation she noticed that in his kitchen there was a ceramic rooster on the counter next to the refrigerator. Ruthie was sure it had been hand painted. In Spain. It would look great on her kitchen table and she wondered if he had any other interesting pieces of furniture she might like.

But the big question was how to murder him. Ruthie took a leap of imagination and brilliance, driving to Montana to visit her father, who had an arsenal of guns in a shed behind his garage. She hadn't seen her father in about ten years and thought it would be best to surprise him. He greeted her in his red long johns, a bottle of Coors in his hand and a cigarette hanging out of the corner of his mouth. The old man took in the sight of her, as if he had just seen her a few hours earlier.

"Come on in. It's colder than a sow's tit out there," he cackled, starting to cough. He watched her struggle with her suitcase and three bags of groceries. He lit another cigarette and watched Ruthie empty all the bags, piling cans and boxes and bananas wherever she could find space in his crowded kitchen. Finally, when she was done, she turned toward him.

Good Riddance, You Commie Bitch

"Hi, Pops. I was wondering if you would like to teach me to shoot." The geriatric coon dog her father had raised from a pup panted and wagged her tail.

"It's okay, Gertie," her father told the dog as he bent down and knuckled her head. "Don't get your bowels in an uproar." He looked up at his daughter. "Why now, all of a sudden, do you wanna learn how to shoot? I thought you was against guns and Republicans." He then reminded her of their last encounter. They had an argument about George Bush and she swore she would never speak to him again. He had yelled "good riddance, you commie bitch" as she slammed his door and drove off.

"Well, that was a long time ago, Pops. I've been reading about the NRA and started thinking about it. My opinions have changed. I think it's important for everyone to have a weapon they know how to use. You know, just in case." Her father eyed her with a mixture of suspicion and delight. Ruthie was a convincing liar. She had practiced it for years.

The next day her father took her out to the firing range and taught her how to load, aim and pull the trigger. Ruthie was a fast learner and after a week she could shoot the cans off the rock ledge almost as good as the old man. In exchange, Ruthie baked him apple pies, gave Gertie a bath and painted his kitchen cabinets dark plum. He bitched about the color but Ruthie convinced him it would grow on him.

If dreaming is planning and planning is doing, Ruthie had already committed the murder. Each night, as she slept in the lumpy old bed from her childhood, with her father snoring across the hallway, she murdered her neighbor. It was a Saturday morning. He was in his backyard mowing the lawn. It had rained and the grass was lush and green and in need of a trim. In her dream, Ruthie hid the small hand gun her father had given her in the pocket of her vest. Because of the noise of the mower, he didn't hear her open the side gate. In her dream, Ruthie shot him in the back of the head. In her dream, she watched him slump forward over the handle of the lawn mower. In her dream, he fell sideways onto the most recently mowed strip of lawn. In her dream, Ruthie entered the house on quiet feet and found Tiger growling under the kitchen table. In her dream, she shot him too. In her dream, Ruthie walked to the painted table, brushed off the keys and the papers and the empty coffee cup, grabbed the table, opened the front door and walked across the street. In her dream, Ruthie took the table to her newly painted bedroom. In her dream, no one had seen her and the man's body was not discovered for three days.

Waiting for the Perfect Moment

Ruthie knew she finally had a foolproof plan. The perfect crime. A premeditated murder? A crime of passion brought on by extreme desire? She knew she was breaking two Commandments (the one about killing and the one about coveting something of your neighbor's). Maybe that made it a double sin. Ruthie had her ways of avoiding those thoughts, by "keeping her eyes on the prize," as they say. She made endless trips to the paint store to bring home small samples of color to try on the walls. She visited linen departments to find the perfect dust ruffle and spent every free minute she could spare watching the house across the street. She was waiting for the perfect moment.

Several weeks after Ruthie returned from her visit to her father in Montana, she came home from shopping and saw an ambulance in the man's driveway and police cars blocking her driveway. Her stomach clenched, just like it did when she was a kid and got caught stealing candy bars from the gas station down at the corner.

"What is going on?" Ruthie asked a cop who was standing close to her driveway.

"You know the guy across the street?" he asked. Ruthie nodded her head, hoping to seem nonchalant.

"Yeah. Kind of. I really don't know him very well. He walks his dog sometimes."

"Well, it's not official yet, but it looks like he had a stroke or a heart attack. Seems he was mowing the lawn and just keeled over. At least that's what it looks like at this point. We're still investigating and looking for clues. You don't happen to know if he has family anywhere, do you?"

"I have no idea. Never saw anyone who looked like family coming by. He does have a dog—a mangy mutty thing."

"Yeah, we found him. He was hiding under the bed. Poor thing was pretty hungry. Shit all over the house. He must not have eaten for a few days. He's looking pretty starved." Ruthie shuddered just thinking about it.

Several hours later, Ruthie watched the ambulance pull away with the man's body. In a few days the obituary turned up in the paper.

Yardley "Yard" Yarborough, 1933–2008. The Lord has seen fit to take Yardley to his bosom. He died peacefully in his garden. Yardley was born to Clyde and Cecily (Pomegranate) Yardley in Fitts, Oklahoma. He graduated from Frothington High School and served in the Korean War. He worked as a machinist until he retired and took up gardening. Mr. Yardley has been preceded in death by his parents, three brothers, two sisters and two wives (Erma and Emma). He is survived by a daughter, Reola Regina Rathington of Las Vegas, New Mexico. There will be no services held and donations in his memory will be accepted by Elks Order 77798, 665 Fergie St.

The Garage Sale

Early Saturday morning, Ruthie awoke to the sound of car doors being closed. When she looked out the front window, she noticed lots of people walking up the driveway of the house across the street. A huge sign outside said GARAGE SALE SAT 7 to 2.

"Oh my God," Ruthie said out loud and quickly put on a pair of jeans and a sweat shirt. When she crossed the street she saw the driveway, lawn and garage filled with furniture, appliances, boxes of tools, books, clothing, shoes, kitchen supplies, bed linens, a television set, an old stereo, cassette tapes, gardening tools…

"Just make an offer. I didn't have time to price anything. I just want to get rid of it all as fast as I can." The woman who said this had salt and pepper hair and wore a knitted poncho from the seventies. She kept repeating herself in a loud voice as she walked through the crowd. Ruthie quickly searched the piles of stuff. She couldn't find it. The table that had almost caused her to commit a heinous crime. She wandered into the garage, pushing her way around disappointed looking people, who seemed to want something to turn into something else. (Nope, it's really just an eggbeater). Ruthie scanned the area searching out the colors of maroon and bright orange. And there, under an enema bag and a box of Depends, Ruthie finally found it. The table to kill for.

Ruthie approached the woman in the poncho, who introduced herself. "My name's Reola. I'm his daughter. I just talked to him about a week ago and he seemed fine and dandy. Didn't complain about anything." She talked about having to sell the house, needing to clear as much out as possible, the truck from the thrift store that would be coming by around 3:00 that afternoon.

After a short negotiation, Ruthie sashayed across the street with the table, and carried it into her awaiting bedroom. The soft orange walls, new fuchsia sheer curtains and the pale yellow-and-black striped comforter seemed to literally glow as she set the small painted table beside her bed. Ruthie stood still for a long time, just taking in the sight. The table, although chipped and a bit wobbly, was now hers. And she got it for a steal. Six bucks.

Ruthie went back across the street, hoping to find the ceramic rooster she had spied in the kitchen. She asked Reola. "Wasn't there a rooster? You know, a ceramic one. I thought I saw one when I was here before."

"Yes. I think some Chinese family took it. Well, I don't know if they were Chinese. Maybe Vietnamese, or Thai. No, wait. I think Filipino, but maybe not." Reola's voice trailed off as she watched a small child putting a very dusty plastic purple grape in her mouth. "Where are her parents? If that child chokes to death, am I supposed to be responsible?"

It was then that Ruthie saw Tiger, looking through the screen door. He looked skinny and old and his eyes had an almost human sadness. To think that she had considered shooting him.

Remember, I Got a Gun and
I Know How to Shoot. So, Watch It, Buddy

Ruthie asked the dead man's daughter what she was going to do with his pitiful dog. "I hate that dog. He's pretty stupid. I guess I'll just take him to the pound. No one would adopt him. They'll probably have to put him to sleep. He was soooooo attached to my dad. Can't imagine him being with anyone else." Tiger eyed them through the door, focusing, it seemed, on Ruthie. His doleful face haunted her and she remembered his soft piles of shit steaming in the cold morning air. "Do you know anyone who might want a pathetic dog?" Ruthie almost stopped breathing, as if something was blocking her windpipe. No, this can't be. Me? With a dog? No fucking way. She shook her head emphatically.

Later that afternoon, after the thrift store truck pulled away from the house across the street, Ruthie saw the woman, still in her ratty poncho, trying to get Tiger in her car. He seemed to be fighting her. Maybe he knew he would be dropped off at the pound. She could hear the woman cursing at him and saw her start to kick him. It was too awful to watch, so she turned and went up to look at her glorious new bedside table.

She waited a month, fighting the urge, but in the end she gave in, telling herself she was simply curious. The man at the front desk told her that they just had too many dogs to take care of, and considering how old and miserable Tiger seemed, they thought it was best to put him out of his misery. "Oh, so he's gone?" Ruthie asked. Relieved.

"Well, today is the day we euthanize. He's in a special holding pen—him and all the others we have to put down." The man picked up a clipboard. "Yup, he's on the list. Too bad. We hate having to do this." Ruthie took a big swallow, which was difficult because of the lump in her throat. Damn, she thought. I was actually willing to kill that mutt just to get a rickety table and now I have it and I keep thinking about that stupid creature. I don't know shit about dogs. Never liked them. Before she knew what she was doing, she banged her hand on the counter. "I'll take him. I'll take Tiger. I can give him a good home. I think he deserves a break."

Three months later...

Tiger and Ruthie had their routine, which was exactly the same routine Tiger had with the old man. Morning walks by the creek, piles of steaming shit near the sycamore. She took him to the neighborhood dog park where Tiger could watch the other dogs romping and sniffing. He was an old man, mostly sitting by Ruthie's side, waiting for her to take him back home. After eight tries, she finally found the kind of food he would eat. Not quite sure how to treat a dog, she thought of him more as a roommate. Or a husband. Of sorts. She read him the newspaper and asked him what he wanted to watch on TV, as if expecting him to answer. "Okay," she'd exclaim and then turn on what she wanted. The dog never liked Dr. Phil, but he seemed to enjoy CSI.

She had her table, which she dusted every Saturday as Tiger sat in the corner, watching her suspiciously. Any time he got out of line, she reminded him, "Remember, I got a gun and I know how to shoot. So, watch it, buddy."

Frosted Petal Pink

The phone rings while Ruthie is lying in bed sucking on a cranberry ice pop. A remarkably hot September night and stifling Santa Ana winds balloon her lace curtains. Already the wind has upset an empty cup from Starbucks and unleashed about a thousand loose pieces of paper. A howling wind fills the room with the smell of hot sand and cactus. Ruthie picks up the phone, but not until she sucks as much cranberry flavor as she can from her gourmet ice pop. It is Fernando calling long distance. She tells him about the Santa Ana and names all the things in her room that have blown against the legs of furniture or simply out the door into the hallway.

"Oh God, my bra just blew under the bed and remember that gold scarf I put over the lampshade? It blew out into the hallway and down the steps and is plastered against the front door." He suggests that she close the window, which is something she hasn't thought of. She gets off the bed and slides the window shut.

"Hey, you were right, it worked." There is absolutely no flavor left in her ice pop, which is now a quickly melting hunk of ice on a stick. "Well, it's good to hear from you. What are you doing?"

"You mean right now?" Fernando is slow on the uptake sometimes. "I'm talking to you, girl. What the hell do you think I'm doing here? Whacking off?"

"What else?" Ruthie asks as she lets the cold drips from the sucked-out ice pop fall onto her thighs.

"Well, let's see. I guess I'm pacing." Ruthie sees Fernando's compact body moving back and forth in his expensive tiny apartment in an overpriced neighborhood. Fernando has a graceful perky walk. She imagines the wall of windows that face the enormous retirement center across the street, where old people sitting in wheelchairs line up on the sidewalk to watch the traffic and wave to drug dealers, who sometimes pimp-walk over to them and shake their hands politely. Fernando lives in the genteel slums of San Francisco. Close to Haight Ashbury.

"What else are you doing? Tell me more." Fernando is silent for a while. Ruthie can hear him inhale deeply. "Are you smoking?"

"Oh yeah, I'm smoking." She asks him what he is smoking and he tells her a Camel Light. "Actually, I've been putting on lipstick because I like the way it looks on the filter."

"Really."

"Yeah, it's kind of fun and silly. Know what I mean? We girls have to be amused, don't we?"

"Where did you get the lipstick?" Outside her window the slender branches of the overgrown pepper tree make wild rustling noises as the wind whips across the yard.

"Oh, let's see. I found it out on the street. I think it was either down in the Castro or perhaps over on Divisidero."

"Are you serious? You're wearing lipstick you found on the street? Are you crazy? Fernando, you could get sick." Ruthie can sometimes not believe Fernando's cavalier attitude towards his health. Along with safe sex, wasn't there something else, like safe lipstick use, or safe cosmetic practices? She imagines a large woman, fresh off the boat coughing with T.B., dropping the tube as she rifles through her purse looking for a bus pass. Or worse yet, a transvestite already infected with HIV, throwing it away because his lips are too covered with lesions to wear lipstick. She imagines any number of things that could have happened to that tube of lipstick, including rabid urban dogs urinating, disease infected rats, a moist toddler with a bad cold fingering and sneezing all over it.

"It's Frosted Petal Pink by Revlon", as if it is a justification to wear it at the risk of his life. "It looks really good against my tan. I've been lying naked out on the roof every chance I get. You should see my tan."

"Fernando, if you want to wear lipstick, why don't you go to Walgreens and buy a new tube? Your own personal tube of lipstick." In spite of her rising anger Ruthie modulates her voice so she sounds like she is talking to the four-year-olds she works with all day. "You see, people's mouths are very dirty. We lick our lips all day long; we touch our lips with our dirty hands. We…"

"Hey, give me a break. Walgreen's doesn't have this color. They said it's discontinued. I'm telling you, girlfriend, don't worry about me." Ruthie is at the point of popping, like a kernel of corn on a hot skillet.

"Okay. I'm serious here, you goddamn Cuban queen. This is serious. Just tell me. Are you really wearing lipstick, and if so, where did you get it?" Fernando lets out a long wet laugh. "No, really, this is not amusing. This is no joke. Just tell me the truth." By now Fernando is howling with laughter. Ruthie waits for him to settle down and catch his breath. "Are you done?" The sound of her voice has apparently sent Fernando into further wails of delight, and she debates whether or not to hang up, but senses that Fernando is coming out of this latest episode of hysterical laughter. He clears his throat several times.

"Oh God, girl, you do make me laugh." His breath heaves from all the strenuous laughter and his voice now sounds strained and distant. Ruthie hates him for having a good time at her expense. "Oh Ruthie, you are so amazingly gullible. What makes you think I would be wearing lipstick I found on the street? Even I wouldn't put on lipstick I found on the street in the Castro. You never know whose disease-infected mouth had been on it. Russian Hill, maybe. But the Castro? Never."

Once more, Fernando is amused enough to break into mild waves of giggles. Ruthie waits for him to calm down. She wants to be sure he can hear what she is about to say. She begins her pontification with a deep breath. "Look, Fernando. I could care less if you wear lipstick, you know that. Whatever rocks your boat, baby. It's the thought of you picking up something off the street and putting in on your mouth. The mouth is sacred. We kiss with our mouth. We eat with our mouth…" Ruthie can hear a distant wheezing sound over the phone and knows that Fernando is being pulled back into another wave of mirth. She stops talking. Fernando clears his throat and asks if she is okay. "Yes, I am fine, and I will no longer bore you with my opinions."

"Thank you, madam. Can we change the subject?" Reluctant to end a diatribe she is just getting into, she agrees to change the subject. "Enough about me," he tells her. "Let's talk about you. So what do you think? Is Frosted Petal Pink my color or should I go for a more mauvy earthy tone?"

Ruthie can't help laughing this time, but it is nothing compared to the endless stream of suppressed giggles she hears on the other end of the phone. She takes her cordless phone and saunters downstairs into the hot kitchen to find another cranberry ice pop. Listening to her friend cackle four hundred miles away, she knows it's going to be a long evening. She's glad Fernando's paying for the call.

"Oh God, I must have needed to laugh. I'm sorry, girlfriend. I've had a shitty day."

"So what happened?" Ruthie is relieved the lipstick episode is over, although she is aware that a snag of the conversation is still lodged in the back of her mind. "Tell me about your bad day." She has come to rely on Fernando's bad days, which are always so much more exciting than her own bad days. She suspects it might be the fact that he lives in a crazy city like San Francisco, where everyone is rushing around "doing things." She lives in Santa Barbara, where people more or less float from one event to the next… a walk on the beach, a business meeting here or there, a lecture, a workshop, an acupuncture session, a surf board repair class, a seascape painting class, a Goddess gathering…

She can hear the flick of a lighter as Fernando lights up another cigarette and she knows that this will be a juicy story. "Wait. Before you tell me, I just want to get one thing clear. You were really just kidding about the lipstick, weren't you? I mean, I want to let this idea go, and if there's the tiniest thought in my mind that you've been wearing orphaned lipstick, it will keep me from being focused on our conversation."

"Ruthie, get over it. Forget the lipstick, okay? I own not one tube of lipstick." She reluctantly accepts this and tells him to go on with his story. "Well, I was riding on the bus this morning. The bus was really crowded, and this young woman was standing like on top of me. She looked like she was in pain and I offered her my seat, but she refused. She was kind of doubling over, and I asked her if she was okay. She didn't seem to speak English - she was Asian. Maybe Chinese or Taiwanese. She kept holding onto her stomach. I was afraid she was about to hurl all over me, which you know has already happened to me on the bus a few times."

In her mind Ruthie pictures Fernando sitting on the seat behind the driver—the long bench that faces the other long bench on the opposite side of the bus, the seats reserved for disabled passengers that anyone can sit in as long as there is no disabled person who needs a seat. She can see a young Asian woman, her face round and pretty, wearing a backpack. "Yeah, go on. I'm with you."

"Well, all of a sudden she doubles over and holds her stomach and starts moaning really loud. I squeeze out of my seat, and sit her down, and she just sits there moaning and rocking back and forth. Someone tells the driver, and he pulls over to the curb. All these people start crowding around. I swear they're like animals up here. Anything for entertainment, you know? The driver keeps telling people to get back, but they just keep pushing closer and closer and finally some woman starts yelling for people to get the fuck back, which seems to work. So this driver asks me if I know anything, and I tell him I have no idea who this woman is, and he keeps asking me 'are you sure you don't know what's wrong with her?' I tell him everything I know, which is very little, but he seems to think I am somehow involved."

"Why did he think you were involved?"

"Aha, this is the clincher. It appears that she's holding onto my hand, but I didn't realize it because of all the excitement in the bus."

"She's holding onto your hand?" Ruthie is totally absorbed now. "Why is she holding onto your hand?"

"Damned if I know. Anyway, by this time most of the people have gotten off the bus to find another one. They've all adopted the Muni stare. You know the look - I'm not really here, it's just my body. The ones who stay are staring out the windows, looking at their cell phones or reading the newspapers, occasionally glancing our way." At this point Fernando starts talking to his cat. Ruthie hates when he does this.

"Hey, go on. Stop with the cat," she whines.

"Oh sorry. Sidney does this thing where he likes to roll all over my dirty clothes in the laundry basket, and..."

"Stop! I want to hear the end of the story."

"Oh yeah. Sorry. So where was I?"

"The part about the Muni stare." Ruthie's second ice pop is half gone. The kitchen is a little cooler than her bedroom upstairs, and she is sitting at the table playing with crumbs from her morning toast. Outside, the hot wind has knocked over all her potted plants.

Fernando is taking his time to get on with the story, which annoys Ruthie, although she knows it's simply part of the suspense. "So anyway," he begins again, "she is squeezing my hand so hard that it's starting to hurt, but I don't want to pull away from her. I can tell how scared she is. The driver, apparently, knows some Chinese and he starts asking her questions, but she keeps shaking her head no. I can't tell if she is answering him or telling him she doesn't understand."

"So what finally happened?"

"Well, what finally happened was that the driver called for an ambulance, but I had to sit with her and hold her hand until the ambulance came. God, it was awful, Ruthie. She was in so much pain and she kept looking at me and saying the same thing over and over and I had no idea what she wanted. I felt so bad. Also I was late for work. Now, this sounds really stupid, and I can't believe

I did this, but I was kind of out of my mind at that point." Ruthie listens, sucking on the last dregs of her ice pop, letting the tart juice slide down her parched throat.

"Yes," she says cautiously. "So tell me…"

"Well, for some crazy reason I start singing to her. I can't believe I did this, but I really did."

"So what did you sing to her?"

"Oh God, this is the weirdest part. Are you ready?" Ruthie is ready. "I started singing Ethel Merman songs to her, like songs from Gypsy - Everything's Coming up Roses, that kind of thing. I felt like I was channeling Ethel. I must have been out of my mind. All those people on the bus just sat with their mouths open. I felt like I was in a Broadway musical." Ruthie is laughing, trying to keep it quiet because Fernando sounds so bewildered.

"Yeah, so what happened next?"

"Well, she seemed to like it, because she stopped yammering and she just stared at me and tried to smile. It was so strange. I've never had anything like this happen before."

"Oh Fernando, you could write a book about your Muni experiences."

"Oh, I know that. But the part about singing? I never sing in public. I can barely manage to sing in the shower because I'm afraid my neighbors will hear me. I have a terrible voice, you know that. I flunked glee club. I just don't know what got into me this morning."

"Fernando, this is good. You did a good thing. This woman will probably never forget you. She'll tell her grandchildren about you. So what finally happened?"

"Well, the paramedics finally got there, but she wouldn't let go of my hand. She had me in a death grip, I swear to God. They had to pry her off me. Then they took her away in the ambulance, and I was too shook up to go to work, so I called in sick and spent the day up on the roof reading."

"Shit, Fernando, that's an incredible story. Did you find out what happened to her? Did you call the hospital?"

"Yeah, I called, but you know the deal. They wouldn't release any information about her because I wasn't a relative. They just said they were holding her for observation."

The Santa Ana winds are still whipping across the yard, like huge clouds of dry scorching heat. She hates these winds. They make her feel like screaming. On the other end of the phone she can hear sirens out on the street and Fernando is having a conversation with one of his cats. He has temporarily forgotten she is on the line. Ruthie can see Fernando still pacing and smoking. She can't help but imagine that his lips have a faint dab of Frosted Petal Pink. She considers asking him, just one more time, to reassure herself that he doesn't, but decides against it and silently listens to him jabbering to his cat in kitty baby talk. "But you know what?"

"No, tell me," replies Ruthie.

"When I got off the bus, after the ambulance took her away?"

"I can't imagine, Fernando. Do tell."

"Everyone on the bus applauded. I mean, like really applauded. Like I was a star or something. Isn't that amazing?"

Ruthie can hear the wind howling outside her window, can feel the heat on the glass. "Well," she says. "It's quite a story. Maybe you should have been wearing that Frosted Petal Pink lipstick."

"I know," replies Fernando. "I was thinking the same thing."

French Widow

My mother's dresser is cherry wood, with a piece of glass cut to fit the top. There are two sets of curved drawers with brass handles. The wood gleams. Under the glass a piece of ivory lace covers the entire top of the dresser. On top of the glass a mirrored tray holds a collection of perfume bottles, makeup, random pieces of jewelry, lipsticks, nail polishes and assorted tiny vials. The mirror over the dresser is unframed and ornately shaped.

As a child, one of my favorite things is to watch my mother get ready to go out to a big event. She sits at her dresser and looks into the mirror to apply her makeup. Her hands are large and her long nails polished and perfect. I sit behind her on her bed, fascinated, as I watch her rub, first, foundation into her skin, then rouge. She uses a round flat puff, to carefully powder her face, concentrating on her high forehead and along the sides of her long narrow nose. For special occasions she pulls her dark hair back into a dramatic bun or a French twist. Sometimes she paints silver streaks in her hair with a tiny brush dipped into a narrow bottle. The silver makes her skin look even darker and her black Rumanian eyes flash in the mirror.

After her makeup, I have to help her into her bustier, a black lace corset that ends at her pubic bone. She calls it a French Widow. Several long garters hang down to her mid thighs. She needs me to help her hitch the tiny hooks that run the front length of the bustier. Together, we count each one as I fasten it. She stops frequently to bend over and lift the French Widow higher and higher until her

89

breasts look like they are sitting on a shelf. The corset pulls her waist tight, giving her the perfect hourglass figure she wants.

The smells of expensive perfume and cigarettes fill the room. My mother usually has a drink with her—something mixed with vodka—and long ribbons of smoke rise from her crystal ashtray. After her French Widow is hooked, she chooses her jewelry for the evening. The top drawer on the right side of her dresser holds enough jewelry to fill a treasure chest, or so it seems to me. My mother loves costume jewelry—good costume jewelry; real rhinestones and intricate marcasite. She has endless rings and dangling bracelets to match long glittering earrings and heavy necklaces. She keeps her best jewelry hidden in boxes underneath her underwear, and when I know she is out of the house, I sneak through her lingerie to find those flat white and gold cardboard boxes, opening each one. Unveiling a treasure.

I watch in fascination as my mother chooses each piece of jewelry, putting on her bracelets, earrings, necklaces. Then she stands in front of the full length mirror, turning from side to side, watching her body move, examining everything. All she wears is her French Widow, stockings, high heels, makeup and her jewelry. The dress or gown she is planning to wear hangs on the closet door, already pressed. Sometimes she wears long dresses covered in sequins, and other times, low cut dresses to show off her lifted breasts. She is beautiful to me, as beautiful as any movie star.

My mother then tells to me to send up my father, who is usually sitting in the living room, all dressed, drinking a high-ball and watching TV. I race down the steps.

"OK Daddy. She's ready."

"Well, it's about time!" He goes up the steps, calling to her: "Lil, are you finally ready? What took you so damn long? You have on that black thing?" I hear the bedroom door open and close. I hear my father laugh. Voices drift down through the ceiling.

When I was younger I felt slighted that I couldn't be in the room with my mother when my father came bounding up the steps. Now I understand that certain things between my parents are private, and I simply wait for them to descend the stairs, put on their coats, grab some packs of cigarettes, and head out the door in a flurry, with a promise to tell me all about their evening the next morning.

The following morning, my mother looks tired, her hair still in the hairnet she wears to bed every night. She tells me what all the women wore. "Dottie Freed wore the cutest blue sequin cocktail dress. You should have seen it. Your Aunt Ronnie had some kind of weird hairdo. She looked like a turnip." My mother is always jealous of her sister, who is even more beautiful than she is.

"Mommy, what did Claire wear?" Claire is her best friend. She has jet black hair and she smokes non-stop. She is about five inches taller than her husband.

"Oh, let me think. Hmmm. Oh yeah. She had on a long red number with a silk jacket that has pearls all along the edge of the sleeves."

"And what about Bernice?" Bernice is married to a man my father plays golf with.

"God, I can't remember. Maybe something gold. George, do you remember what she wore?" My father looks perplexed. "Oh come on. You danced with her about five times. You must remember what she was wearing." She lights another cigarette to have with her cup of black coffee.

"Lil, I don't pay any attention to what your friends wear. How should I know? I danced with her. I didn't inspect her outfit." Then he tells me that my mother was the most beautiful woman there. They drink coffee and smoke and complain about headaches. My father touches my mother a lot the morning after these events. Then he runs off to play 18 holes of golf and my mother bitches about it. It's always the same.

Town and Country

I dedicate this story to Alan Dawson

1967

It is the summer before my junior year of college. My boyfriend Ronnie is in the army, waiting to be sent to Vietnam, and I am spending the summer at home in Ohio with my parents. My father has threatened to kill me if I don't find a job. He and my mother have no compassion for my anguish over Ronnie. I am unsure whether my father would actually kill me if I don't find a job. True or not, I don't want to find out.

In desperation for work, I change the date of my birth on my driver's license. This is before the days of laminated licenses. All I need is a typewriter and some Liquid Paper. Now I can get a job serving alcoholic drinks. With my amended driver's license, I land a job waitressing at Town and Country Restaurant.

Town and Country is a huge establishment with an enormous buffet of every bland starchy food known to man. The buffet line runs about 30 feet down the middle of the main dining room. The décor consists of dim lighting, linen table cloths and napkins, a gleaming bar and mountains of food artistically displayed, creating an ambiance of lushness. It is a favorite stop for people who like lots of cheap mediocre food, which pretty much describes the entire population in town.

Besides waitressing, I commute 60 miles a day to my university to attend summer classes. Each morning, my friend Alan, who is a high school drama coach with dreams of becoming a Broadway actor, picks me up. He is also taking some classes. My mother met Alan doing theatre work and he and I have become good friends. Our friendship is based on going to bars at night, drinking girlie drinks (sloe gin fizzes, Mai Tais, and daiquiris) and making each other laugh hysterically. We go to bars where Alan knows the waiters, so I don't have to show my ID.

My schedule is incredibly tight. Up at 7:00, picked up by Alan by 7:30, classes at the university from 8:30 to 11:30, home by 12:30 and then off to waitress from 3:00 to 11:00. There is little time to do homework and every night I have to wash my only waitress uniform by hand and hang it to dry for the next day.

My job basically consists of taking drink orders, after which I direct people to the buffet line. I then go to the bar, where the beverages for each table are placed on round trays, which I then take back to the tables to distribute. Unfortunately, I can never remember which table ordered which round tray of beverages, plus I am totally unfamiliar with mixed drinks and can't tell a shot of vodka from a shot of scotch from a shot of gin or a shot of bourbon. Generally, I place the tray on the table and let the customers pick out their own drinks. Most of the time customers don't seem to mind, but occasionally they get pissy and refuse to leave a tip.

The price of unlimited trips to the buffet is $2.50. At this time (the 1960's), gratuities are 10% of the tab, which means that tips don't amount to much unless the table runs up a big bar tab. Then, it's a gamble whether people will even remember to leave a tip. Some leave enormous tips and others are so drunk they walk out, failing to pay for anything. After two parties stiffed me with their bill, I learned to keep a close watch on my customers. The whole affair is very dicey.

After the busboys clear the table, each waitress has to run for clean linen and totally redo the table for the next party of questionable tippers. There is a vague rule about when to replace the white table cloth and when to simply put down a linen napkin to cover up a small stain. I never seem to get it right.

Sometimes my customers ask me to serve them. I have a difficult time remembering anything more complicated than "could you get me another small piece of prime rib with gravy and another scoop of mashed potatoes with no gravy." Sometimes I am requested to "find me an end of pork roast with no fat on it, and if it's not very big, how about some beef stew, but leave out the carrots and potatoes and also some of those green beans mixed with carrots, but leave out the carrots and, if you don't mind, a large helping of sauerkraut, but in a separate bowl. Oh, and another roll with butter, not margarine, and a little bit of that macaroni and cheese, but don't put it next to the beef stew because I don't want the gravy... well, just put the mac and cheese in a separate bowl." Yeah, right. Like I have three hands. These are usually the assholes who neglect to leave a tip.

The best part of working at Town and Country is that before the restaurant is opened, the entire staff gets to eat as much as we like and throughout the night we are allowed to grab snacks from the table. I gain at least ten pounds while working there. My favorite is the hard crusty home-made rolls with pats of real butter. My mother uses only margarine, which tastes like plastic.

The other waitresses are mostly middle-aged women who have been waiting tables since they were in their teens. These are tough women, who get into fist fights over a favored customer. The hostess, who seats the parties, walks a fine line. She must be careful not to sit Norma Sue's big tipper in Mary Jean's station. All the waitresses have bleached blond hair, smoker's coughs and two names—Betty Ann, Linda Ray, Linda Sue, Mary Sue, Mary Ann, Mary Pam, Peggy Sue, Peggy Jean, Louise Ann, Mary Jo, Peggy Jo. Each carries a pack of cigarettes in the pocket of her apron and one of those flippy silver lighters that make a metal singing noise.

We take breaks in the back of the restaurant out by the trash cans. They all look like milk-maid prostitutes with their ratted bleached hair and bright-red lipstick in their Town and Country uniform—a pink nylon full skirted pinafore over a puffy sleeved pink blouse, and a ruffled pink apron tied around the waist. I wear a white nylon nurse's uniform because this is a summer job and I refused to buy the whole pink get-up. I made the mistake of telling the other waitresses that I will be returning to the university in the fall. They eye me with distrust, as if going to college is somehow suspect. "So, what are you gonna be when you get your paper?"

"My paper?"

"Yeah, you know. Your paper from college?" Peggy Lou spits out the word "college" the same way she spits out tiny pieces of tobacco that get stuck on her tongue.

"My diploma?"

"Whatever you wanna call it."

"Well, I plan to be a teacher." I shrug when I say this, as if it's something I'm a little ashamed of. Like, if I really had ambition and was smarter, I would aim for a career as a waitress.

Peggy Lou takes a long drag off her Kent, raises her eyebrows and glances at the other waitresses standing around the coffee can we all use to throw our butts into. "Hmmm. That's real nice. Real nice." I look for a friendly face. They all turn, as if choreographed, and return to the dining room to grovel for tips.

My father waits for me to come home each night and helps me count my tips. We separate all the coins and he adds it up in his head. "Hey, twenty-five bucks. Not bad." My biggest night is Saturday when I come home with a whopping 50 or 60 bucks. He is so happy he pours me a highball. He knows that I changed my birth date on my driver's license to get this job. He keeps reminding me that if I get caught serving alcohol the restaurant owner and I will be in big trouble and may end up in jail. The other thing he keeps reminding me is that the owner is a known anti-Semite.

"If anyone asks you, tell them you're Italian. Whatever you do, don't admit you're Jewish."

"But Dad, I look totally Jewish and have a Jewish last name."

"Hey, the goyim don't know from Jewish names. We could be Italian Jews. Just do something with your hair." I never heard of Italian Jews. This whole situation is making me very nervous. The cops that come in for dinner every night, the Jewish thing, my boyfriend going to Vietnam, my university classes… I'm losing sleep over all this.

The busboys are cute, mostly Italian or Irish guys who go to Central Catholic High School. They are nice, and sniff around me when I walk by the dish room. Sometimes one of them will say something like: "Hey, did I see you in church the other day?"

"I don't know. What church would that be?"

"St. Mike's."

"Oh, really? I didn't see you." Over the course of the summer I have hinted at going to St. Mike's, Our Lady of Sacrifices, St. Sebastian's, First Baptist, Unitarian Society, Church of the Redeemer, the Greek Orthodox Church and Eastside Methodist.

The owner of the Town and Country (the anti-Semite) sometimes hovers over me, especially before we open the doors to the public, when I have to sit at the bar and fold napkins. He always wears dark shiny suits and highly polished black shoes. His hair seems to gleam from all the Brylcreem he puts in it. When I tell my friend Alan about him, I call him Mr. Shimmer because of his almost blinding shininess. Mr. Shimmer asks me a lot of questions but doesn't seem to really be interested in my answers.

"How are you today, honey? Did you just wash your hair? It smells good. What did you do on Saturday? How's it goin'?" He lights my cigarettes and I keep waiting for him to ask me which church I go to. Maybe he wants to see my driver's license. His attention makes me extremely nervous and I fold the linen napkins backwards and he keeps leaning over to show me how to fold them correctly. His breath smells like cigarettes and alcohol.

I can't wait for the summer to be over, for school to start, for Ronnie to finally be in Vietnam so I don't have to go through the stress of waiting. The waiting is killing me. The bitchy waitresses are mean to me. The restaurant owner is starting to touch my hair and the busboys are starting to ask me out. A few cops show up every night for dinner and it is making me very nervous. I hate my uniform, which is too tight after all those rolls and butter.

I convince my parents never to show up for dinner on a night I'm working, but my friend Alan insists. He promises he won't embarrass me or make me laugh or wear a silly hat or anything. One night he shows up wearing a sports coat that is about three sizes too small. This I can deal with as long as he pretends not to know me. He is, thank God, seated at Mary Pat's table, on the other side of the vast dining room. Alan spends an inordinately long time at the restaurant this evening. He makes about five trips to the dessert bar. Alan likes to eat. I keep an eye on him and he gives me little finger waves as he makes stupid faces.

As a part of the job, I must carry huge trays of glasses from the dish room and slide them into a high cart that sits in the station where the coffee and tea supplies are kept for my section of the dining room. The job is tricky, as the trays are heavy and hard to balance, but after a few weeks I feel confident that I have the hang of it. As I lift a tray over my head to slide into the cart, it becomes unbalanced and, as if in a dream, falls to the floor, breaking every glass and making a thunderous crashing noise. Everyone in the restaurant turns their head to look. There is a moment of silence and then applause.

I turn to watch Alan trying not to laugh, holding his hands in front of his mouth, his body starting to shake until he can't help himself anymore. He howls with laughter. Absolutely howls! Everyone, at some point, drops a tray of glasses. I am now an official member of the staff.

That night when I walk in the door at 11:30, I find Alan and my parents sitting in the living room. My parents attempt to act normal, trying to suppress their laughter, but I can see them starting to deteriorate into giggles. Eventually, we all end up in hysterics as Alan describes the whole fiasco of me dropping an entire tray of glasses and then he sits down at the piano and plays the entire medley from Oliver, his favorite musical. We all sing along between fits of laughter.

The Landscape of Aphrodite's Body

The boy has been awake since the first beams of the sun melted across the sky. He is waiting. The shape under the blue woolen blanket shifts slightly, like small earthquakes snaking across the mountains. In his warmest flannel pajamas, stained with grape juice, the boy crouches beside her body, his back against the cold wall, listening to the chatter of birds greeting the sun and foraging for food. He hears the baby goats bleating for their mothers' milk.

He drives his small green truck over the hills and valleys of his mother's body. The protruding crest of her wide hip marks the apex of the landscape, then the long decline of her thigh until the ridge takes a turn at her knee, slanting farther and farther down to the lump of her ankle, until the truck is on the flat plains of the bed.

He is content to drive his truck back and forth across his mother. Sometimes he takes it across the ridge of her bent arm, over the summit of her shoulder and deep into the valley of her clavicle, avoiding the jungle of her black hair, as this will awaken her. He knows from past experience that he is never to awaken her before she is awakened by the kiss of the Goddess. The Goddess protects them both. He knows this because his mother told him that the Goddess shelters them as they sleep. His mother kisses the small icon on the table next to her bed each night before she goes to sleep and gives thanks for the blessing of another day.

As the room lightens in the misty winter sun, colors begin to emerge—blue bowls sitting along a ledge, golden brown of an old wooden bench and the red and green pillows along the bench. The room is cold and his feet are icy. Still, he waits.

His mother sighs and moves and his green truck tumbles onto the tiled floor. It makes a clacking sound as it falls and for a few seconds the child sits as still as a statue. He is afraid he has awakened her. The landscape of her body resettles itself under the blue blanket, offering the child new hills and valleys to explore with his truck.

The mother is dreaming of the sea. She watches gulls circle the shore, waiting for the fishermen to dock their boats. She dreams of vast nets and the repairing of them in front of the fire each night. She dreams of a picnic—fresh feta, crusted bread and a dark bottle of red wine.

His mother's name is Aphrodite, the same as the Goddess. She has told him that she is not a Goddess, just a simple woman. He thinks she has lied to him about this. He believes, in his tender seven-year-old heart, that his mother is none other than the Aphrodite of the icon beside her bed. He thinks she is lying to him because if she told him the truth he would talk about it in the village square and then everyone would bother her for blessings. This is a secret he will hold in the deepest part of his soul for several more years.

Aphrodite, deep in her dream, hears the sound of silver waves hitting the beach. She smells the stink of rotting fish threaded through the aroma of roasted lamb and seaweed. In her dream, her lover walks toward her. His skin is dark and his black hair shines in the bright Mediterranean light. Behind him, the vast sea has turned turquoise. They make love in a white hut with the sound of gulls just outside the arched doorway. In her dream they are married. To each other.

The child, whose name is Nicolo, tries to match his breaths to those of his mother. He puts his face a few inches from hers and breathes her familiar scent—olive oil and candle wax and something fresh, perhaps cucumbers and mint. This is the aroma that sooths him when he is sick or unhappy. After listening a while, he is able to discern her inhalation and exhalation, the shimmering movement of her chest. He imitates her breath, slowing his own down until he is lying beside her, breathing her essence, as he did when he was a small fish floating inside her waters. His mother tells him when he is a big boy he will someday want to leave her, but he believes that this will never happen. A piece of the chord that connected them when he was growing inside her still remains, as fine as a spider web, just one strand, luminescent and tied to his navel.

They live now in a small village in the mountains, far away from the sea. He has never known any other place than this. Aphrodite has photographs of the fishing village on the edge of Santorini, where she grew up and where Nicolo was conceived. She tells him stories of her childhood, of her older brothers who went out every day in boats to net kilos of fish. Her father died at sea and the brothers had to keep the family fed. She tells him about the black sand beaches and describes the curling sea horses that float into the harbor. She talks dreamily of the caldera where a huge volcano formed the crescent shaped island thousands of years ago

There are photographs of a small dark man. His teeth are very white and he smiles with his mouth open, as if he is laughing. Nicolo knows this man is his father. When his mother isn't looking, he stands on a stool in front of the mirror and tries to make his face look like the face of the man in the photos. He holds his head up, thrusts one shoulder back and forces himself to laugh with his mouth open. There. I can do it too, he tells himself. I am the son of this man.

In the room, now filled with hazy mountain light, Nicolo's stomach growls from hunger. He craves warm milk from the goats. He has a taste for yogurt and bread. Kneeling beside his mother on the bed, he blows into her ear, moving the ringlets of her black hair with his over-zealous breath.

Aphrodite opens her eyes suddenly, as if startled. "Mama," he says, "I woke you up. It was an accident. I was trying to, to…" The mother pulls herself up and wraps the blanket around her shoulders. She reaches out to the child, who moves toward her slowly. She grabs him, pulls his body into her lap and wraps the two of them inside her blanket, making a tent that covers them both.

"No, my little man, you didn't wake me. The Goddess whispered in my ear that you are hungry. It was she who woke me." Aphrodite kisses her son's shoulder. She feels his small truck driving through the darkness, inside their deep blue tent, across the landscape of her body. Thru the blanket he can hear her questions. "Are you hungry? Yes? Shall I get you something to eat? Yes? I have figs and apricots and some pistachios. You like?"

Morning Has Broken

I have woken up early and am out of my tent. It is the breaking of dawn, in total quietude, the eastern sky showing smears of pink clouds like shreds of silk. Birds rustle the trees, which hover over our campsite. The huge bay and oaks spread their arms, forming a net of protection. Below the cliff, the stream reflects the light in the sky and it sparkles in the silent morning. No cars, no radios, no airplanes flying over. It's a sweet Sunday morning at the end of yet another blessed weekend.

I am camping with a group of musicians. We do this every summer, as often as possible. We gather together under the trees, somewhere in California, usually the central coast or at various music festivals. We make music, we cook, we eat, we laugh and share our gifts. We swap stories and talk of past gatherings, but mostly we share our love of all kinds of music. I seem to be the only one awake and out of my tent. I can hear a whisper of distant snores and snorts. Other than that, no one seems to be stirring. I take the five-minute walk up to the bathhouse, which has actual flush toilets and hot water showers.

When I come back, I put myself in a reclining camp chair, cover myself with a quilt and just listen to the sounds. I feel almost invisible this morning. I hear movement inside tents. The cacophony of early morning coughers, like music coming from all directions. Distant rumblings of people waking up, moving around, zipping and unzipping sleeping bags and tents. The sound of water boiling on the camp stove. The aroma of bacon, the cracking of eggs. Throat-clearing sessions, grunts and belches and farts. The sound of old men greeting the day. Laughter. Footsteps and the crunching of leaves. Matt and Oscar talk about the potato pancakes they are preparing. And of course, the usual recitations regarding the amazing wonders of bacon. Something sizzles in the pan, sounding almost like a gentle drizzle. If only it were true. This land would be so grateful. The water in the creek is at the lowest level anyone has seen in over 50 years. The hills around us are golden and dry as a match, just waiting for a spark to explode. We are reverent, all of us.

Yesterday, for the first time ever, I sang loud enough for others to hear. It has always been my dream to be a singer. I know I can carry a tune, but I get extraordinarily shy if anyone is listening. I sometimes stand with the few women in our camp and we harmonize. I put my hands over my ears, so I can hear my own voice. I sing almost in a whisper. But yesterday something inside me broke open, like a baby chick coming out of its shell. And I let my voice be heard. And it was okay that I was sometimes off tune. I didn't let that stop me. I sang. Out loud. For everyone to hear.

With my eyes still closed, I hear coffee-making sounds. A whistling tea kettle. Men yawning and grumbling and chuckling. They made music until very late. Some of them only slept two or three hours and sound, still, as if they were partially asleep. They stumble and smile and complain of aching backs. They are happy. We have spent almost three days together making music. And then I can hear the women starting to wake up. Soft laughter. Tooth brushing, pots of water boiling.

My tribe is waking up around me. This is the tribe that called to me over twenty years ago, when I accompanied my brother to one of these gatherings. I had no idea what I was getting myself into. I just trusted him and let him park me in a borrowed tent along the creek while he and his friends made music. And I watched. And I listened. I knew my brother played the harmonica, but I had no idea. My brother and I grew up in a family of musicians. Our mother was a trained pianist and her beautiful hands flew across the ivory keyboard. Classical, popular, Broadway tunes. She loved it all. Her favorite composer was Rachmaninov. There was always music in the background. With the grandparents and aunts and uncles and cousins, our most fun activity was to stand around the piano and sing together.

When my brother and the other musicians were done making music, they sat down for a few hours of poker, marijuana and beer. I was left to wander and find quiet places where I could be silent and simply listen to nature. I sat by the creek, watching the leaves float over the rocks below. The water so clear, sparkling in the sun. As it rushed down the creek, it carried bits of leaves and sticks and small insects. I tried to stay focused on the rocks beneath the clear water. They never moved. I suddenly understood meditation. It is noticing the leaves go by while having a single pointed focus. That bright light that dwells within each of us. Consciousness is a flowing river. Crystal clear.

And when I started to feel lonely, I simply wandered and met other people. We shared our stories and found each other around the nightly campfire, where all the musicians came to share the joy of making music. Together. In cooperation. Under the sheltering trees. All supporting and honoring each other's gifts. They encouraged each other and forgave the mistakes. With their guitars, with their horns, with harmonicas, with percussion, with violins and mandolins and ukuleles and washtub bases alongside beautifully polished instruments and the dreaded banjos. They jammed into the wee hours of the morning. It was pure joy to watch, to listen, to feel.

Now, twenty years later, we have grown old together. We continue to return, to share music and stories and meals and so much laughter. We all vow that we will return as long as we are able to get our asses here. And each time I drive away from these gatherings, I am grateful and my heart is filled. And I am happily very dirty, aching for a shower and already looking forward to the next gathering.

Annabel Embraces the Day

It had been almost eight months since Delia died. Porter still awoke each morning slightly startled to see the empty space beside him in the bed. It was not a sudden death. And even though he had been beside her, watching the dark storm breathe through her body, taking away parts of her until there was nothing left, it seemed that one morning she had simply disappeared. Like all those people in Argentina or Chile he read about. Disappeared.

Porter was still finding remains of Delia's existence. Painful reminders. Photographs of her popped up in odd places—the pocket of his old jacket, at the bottom of his tackle box. Her comb appeared behind the toilet one day, and her blond hairs still clung to the backs of the couch cushions no matter how many times he vacuumed them away. Occasionally, he would find a pair of her panties in with his socks. He sometimes suspected that she intentionally placed reminders of herself all over the house to ensure that he not forget her.

Delia had a habit of placing yellow Post-It notes in unexpected places... on the dashboard of his car, on the bathroom mirror, the kitchen window, the front door...

Call Dr. T. today

Margaret's birthday

Paint thinner

40-watt bulbs

When she was alive, Porter barely noticed the small yellow squares but now, each time he came across one, it took his breath away, especially to read his own name...

Porter dentist 3:30

Port call Steve W

Porter in Chicago 12/2–12/14

Ever since Delia's death, Porter took an early morning walk before leaving for work, to lubricate his aching bones. He liked the feel of clean cool air in his lungs as he watched the sky fill with light. He enjoyed the quiet, the serene atmosphere when most people were still asleep or just waking up. He felt his joints loosen, his abdomen relax. One morning, while taking a slightly different route, he thought he noticed a naked woman through the slats of a wooden fence. To make sure, he retraced his steps back to the edge of the fence and walked past it again, this time going slower and looking more closely at the scattering image through the redwood boards.

Porter could tell she was not a young woman, perhaps his own age; her skin dark from sun exposure, her legs slender, and her stomach softly rounded. Her yard was lush with orange and loquat trees, hibiscus, and oversized fuchsia bushes. He recognized a traditional yoga pose. Delia had, for several years, watched an early morning yoga program on the television. Porter enjoyed sitting on the couch drinking coffee as his wife stretched her tall lanky body into what seemed impossible contortions. Occasionally he attempted to beguile her with sexual comments. "Oh Baby, I'm comin' to get you right now. I wanna jump your yoga bones." Delia usually shooed him away, trying not to laugh.

Porter got home from his morning walk, drank several glasses of water, and when he put the glass back into the cupboard he spotted a silver ring shoved into the far back corner. He had never noticed this ring before, but he knew it must have been Delia's. He sensed the ring had a story. She had been reluctant to talk about certain things, claiming that she had to retain parts of her past, as if revealing them would somehow diminish her. Porter sensed that she sometimes used her silences to entice him.

In the ten years they were together Porter lived with an

intermittent yearning to know his wife in a deeper way. The only relief from this yearning occurred when they made love, when he became so caught up in his own sensations, in the closeness of his wife's presence, that everything else seemed to disappear. In those moments he lost track of himself, not knowing whose body he was in, not caring. He often wished they could trade corporeal space. That he might project himself inside D's body, looking at himself through her eyes. To him, this would be the epitome of intimacy.

"It's not so horrible that I'm dying before you, Port. If I had lived too long, we might end up like all those couples we know who basically don't like each other anymore. Just don't forget me, okay? And mourn properly. At least two weeks." These were her last lucid words, spoken in a breathless whisper through her dry cracked lips, her smile cunning. Porter forced a chuckle, knowing that was what his wife expected of him. But now there were times when he couldn't release his resentment that even in her last days she held back, kept her cards close to her chest, not revealing any distress at her own impending death. How dare she be so cavalier about the whole dying thing?

After several days Porter was able to time his morning walks so that he could observe the naked woman doing her sun salutations, her body upright, welcoming the morning. He experimented to find the exact pace that would allow him the most optimal view of her straight back and small drooping breasts being pulled up by her reaching arms, which seemed to embrace the morning sky, the air. Embraces the Day. He called her that, imagining they were members of an Indian tribe, perhaps the Spokane or Shoshone. His name would be Likes to Peek, or Walks by Fences. Porter Walks by Fences. He imagined her real name as lyrical and melodic. Annabel. Annabel Embraces the Day.

Porter awoke each morning anticipating a glimpse of her, expecting her always to be standing in the sun with her arms pointing towards the sky, still and beautiful in her calmness. He imagined her as an artist, a grandmother, in a house filled with cages of singing canaries and plastered child-sized handprints.

One morning Porter found Annabel's yard empty. He became concerned that something had happened to her; sudden death, a hangover, a migraine. Later that day there was a letter in his mailbox addressed to Mrs. Delia Porter. It was hand addressed, obviously personal, and he debated whether or not to open it, or scrawl "deceased" and stick it back in the box. He was sure it was a man's handwriting, and the postmark was from somewhere in Wyoming. Although he had never been jealous of his wife, he was endlessly curious about the details of the life she lived before he met her. He opened the letter and read a short message from a man named Cody D, who talked about having fun together in Acapulco "back when we were all hippies and the tequila was cheap." Cody D. hoped she was well and happy and implored her to keep in touch. There was no return address and Porter tossed the letter into the trash.

It amazed Porter how easily he could obtain information through simple observation; the name on her mailbox (Farnell), her telephone number in the book. Annabel Farnell? It didn't sound right. Besides, the phone book listed her as C. Farnell. Cynthia, Candace, Clarice, Carla, Catherine, Clyde, Calvin, Clothild? He preferred to think of her as Annabel—Annabel Embraces the Day. He drove by her house—buzzed her, as he and his high school friends had called it. Buzzing consisted of driving by the house of a girl you were interested in, both hoping and dreading to see her out on the front porch. He buzzed Annabel Embraces the Day's house several times a week, hoping to see her out in the yard, getting her mail, pulling weeds. He wanted to know what she looked like in clothes.

Delia had been his third wife, and he promised himself when he married her that this time it would work. The first two wives, he decided, had been practice. He felt that Delia was the one he had been waiting for all his life. When, at age 53, he met her, he believed that marrying a younger woman would somehow protect him from his greatest fear—growing old alone. When she was diagnosed with cancer, more than dread or the anticipation of loss, he felt cheated; tricked by some evil plan. Hadn't he stopped drinking, smoking dope, gambling, going to prostitutes? Hadn't he become a model husband, ridding his life of excesses, devoting himself to a woman who had willingly given up her own wildness? If only he could accept that life follows its own path. That destiny hovers over us, and that other people were continuing to live lives unfazed by tragedy or loss. Porter knew he was prone to sentiment, and struggled with his tendency to dramatize his wife's death and the fact that his life had gone on without her. Death is a fact of life, he kept telling himself. How many tears can one shed?

Evenings were the most difficult time for Porter. Inside the quiet house, the aroma of barbeques and the chatter of neighborhood children's voices drifted through his open windows as he sat imagining that everyone else in the world had someone by their side to share the evening with. His loneliness felt like swimming in a cold dark lake, unable to see the shore. Occasionally Porter had lunch with work acquaintances or dinner with one of his grown children, who talked about him to each other, in hushed tones. Words like "depression, wallowing, medication, stuck, obsessing, needs an outlet, grieving takes time…" He sensed their concern, their focusing on his so-called dilemma, and it shamed him to think that people saw him as a tragic figure, an object of pity. He preferred to spend his time alone, sitting in a dark room listening to jazz, drinking iced tea and looking at old Playboy magazines and smoking. Cigarettes were the one vice he returned to after Delia's death.

Sometimes at night Porter took long walks, making sure that he passed by the home of Annabel Embraces the Day. Her curtained windows gave off an apricot glow, conveying a sense of warmth and privacy. Porter ached to know what was behind those drapes, who she was with, what she was doing. One night he snuck down the driveway of an empty house directly behind hers, entering the backyard where he thought he might be able to observe her. He found several knotholes in the fence, which offered him a series of rounded views into her world.

Through one hole he could see into the kitchen, where her countertops appeared to be cluttered with bowls. He imagined these were ceramic pots that she had made many years before, when she was a potter, when her name had been Annabel Throws Pots and she had been surrounded by children reaching up to her; children who held the memory of being suckled by her soft milk-filled breasts.

Through another knothole he saw into her bedroom through an open sliding glass door. The light in the room was on and he could see the edge of her bed and a table. He waited. Eventually the phone rang and she walked into the bedroom to pick up. She faced the glass door, looking at her own reflection. Her hand went up to her hair, rearranging it as she talked on the phone. He watched her stretch her body, arch her back, raise herself up on her toes, bend at the waist, all the time speaking in a low voice. Occasionally she laughed. Annabel Embraces the Day wore a long summer nightgown too large for her frame. She was ageless at this distance, anywhere from forty to sixty. Her voice was strong and her laugh had a depth that seemed to vibrate inside Porter's chest.

He watched her sit on the edge of her bed talking on the phone, holding the receiver between her ear and a raised shoulder as she bent over to put on a pair of white socks. Eventually she hung up, placed the phone on the dresser and flipped off the light. Porter walked home through the dark streets filled with a sense of anticipation, his skin covered with a sheen of nervous perspiration.

The first time he telephoned, Porter hung up as soon as Annabel Embraces the Day answered. Embarrassment heated his body and he felt his heart pound. Afterwards, he smoked three cigarettes in a row to calm himself. After so many years of marriage, he had lost his old ease with women. He felt young, not physically, but socially; awkward, like a seventeen-year-old calling his first girlfriend. He pulsed with anticipation and walked away from the phone into the garage to check his laundry, where he picked up a bottle of bleach.

The white plastic container was empty, and attached to the bottom he found a yellow Post-it that read "What does Porter want for his b-day?" The day before, he had found a note that simply said Fuck u. He looked up into the rafters, imagining Delia hovering over him laughing.

"It's been more than two weeks, Baby," he called into the space above him. That night he had a difficult time getting to sleep, and when he did, he dreamed of Delia out in the back eating pebbles and coughing them up into her hand, which she offered to him. When he woke up in the morning his head ached and he stayed in bed too long to walk before work.

The next time he called her, Porter was in a Chicago hotel room. The distance somehow made him feel safer. He was on a business trip and after a grueling day of meetings he wanted to be back home, sitting in the dark with his Miles Davis CD and a cold drink. He had just returned from dinner with a former lover, a woman he had always found bitter. She seemed to be aging poorly, her skin loose and unhealthy looking. He imagined it was all those years of breathing polluted air. It made him think of Delia at the end of her life, when she seemed to fade like an old photograph, becoming less and less substantial, yet more beautiful in a strange ethereal way. Cancer had drained her of her sharp edges, softening everything about her.

Porter's hand shook slightly as he dialed Annabel Embraces the Day's phone number from his hotel phone. After three rings an answering machine picked up. "Sorry I missed your call, but please leave a message and I'll call you back as soon as I can. Have a good day." The message revealed nothing about her personal life and he was disappointed, yet enthralled by her voice. Annabel Embraces the Day's speech was absent of any accent he could discern. He thought of the things he was glad he didn't hear on her message. She didn't say a man's name or use the word "we." That night he had a difficult time sleeping. He kept hearing her voice in his head.

He felt absolutely adolescent and stupid.

The next morning when Porter was packing to leave Chicago and fly home he found a crumpled note from Delia in his suitcase. "Port, I'll miss you." Bring me something wonderful from N.O. Don't forget to take your antibiotic and keep warm. Call me. Don't worry, I forgive you. "Just don't do it again." He couldn't remember ever reading the note, although he must have been the one who balled it and stuck it deep into the side pocket. It made him wonder how many other things about her he had forgotten. N.O. was how they referred to New Orleans, but he had no memory of which trip, or what he had done that required forgiveness. It could have been any number of transgressions—a hurtful comment, forgetting to call, a display of temper.

Delia had a tendency to imagine infidelities, betrayals. Porter was often shocked to come home and find her in tears over something she had misinterpreted—a call from another woman, a comment made by his secretary that he was too busy to come to the phone, a forgotten anniversary. It angered him that she was so suspicious when he was, after all, faithful to her beyond his own belief. He eventually regretted being so truthful about his previous affairs and flirtations.

Porter became obsessed with thoughts of Annabel Embraces the Day. One afternoon at work, alone in his office, he dialed her number.

"Hello?" She sounded surprised, interrupted.

"Yes. Is Albert there?"

"Albert? I'm sorry, but you must have the wrong number. There's no Albert here." Porter repeated her number back to her." Yes, that's my number, but I don't know anyone named Albert."

"I'm sorry, ma'am. I hope I haven't disturbed you. Apparently, I wrote down the wrong number." He had rehearsed his lines and felt confident. He told himself he just wanted to hear her voice.

"No, it's quite alright. I hope you find Albert," her manner gentle and concerned.

"Well, I'll have to do some more research. I am sure this was the number I was given." Porter felt the conversation ending and wanted desperately to keep her on the line. "May I ask you if you have had this number for a long time? Perhaps, if it's a new number, it might have been Albert's number previously."

"I'm afraid I've had this number for many years. I wish I could be of more help to you. Good luck."

"Oh, I'm afraid it will take more than luck. It will take perseverance, but I'm very persistent when I need to be." God, he thought, what a ridiculous thing to say. There was silence on the other end of the phone. "I hope I didn't disturb you."

"Well, I was involved in something. It's okay. I needed to take a break anyway." He heard water running in the sink. He heard her swallow a few gulps and waited for her to finish.

"You have been very patient, ma'am. May I ask your name?"

"My name is Farnell. You have a good day."

"Thank you, Mrs. Farnell—excuse me, but is it Miss or Mrs.?"

"Mrs."

"Oh, then you're married?" Porter felt heat creep up his spine.

"No, I am no longer married. I hope you locate your friend."

"Oh wait, don't hang up yet. I hear some birds. Do you have canaries by any chance?"

"Excuse me? Canaries? No, I would never keep birds in cages. I have three cats. They would eat them in no time flat."

"Cats," he exclaimed with way too much enthusiasm. "I have cats," he lied. "I am a cat person, like yourself."

"Well, I don't know if I would call myself a cat person. I simply have three cats that I feel obliged to feed. They live outside, mostly, except for Guido. He's an orange tabby. He likes to sleep on the couch."

"This is quite amazing. I have an orange tabby myself. Her name is Sam... Samantha. Yes, Samantha is quite the cat."

"A female orange tabby? I've never heard of that. I thought orange tabbies were always males."

"Well yes, so did I until I found Samantha. She's very masculine, actually. For a long time I thought she was a male. But someone pointed out to me that she was a female. Very strange. By the way, my name is Porter. It's been very nice talking to you, and I am sorry to have disturbed you."

"It was no bother. I assure you. Well, goodbye, Mr. Porter." Annabel Embraces the Day hung up the phone. Porter felt foolish. He had started to perspire and the odor of his nervousness filled the small office. He walked to an open window and lit a cigarette, taking a deep puff and holding it inside his lungs as long as he could, until his head began to swim. The exhale made him cough so harshly that his throat felt raw. Good, he told himself. You deserve it after you lied like that. A cat named Samantha, please. Porter felt sick and went home early.

That night he took a walk by Annabel Embraces the Day's house. All the lights were out except for the porch light, and her car was gone. He stood on the sidewalk smoking, hoping to see one of the cats she felt obliged to feed. Inside the house he heard a phone ring three times. The machine must have picked it up. He tried to remember the words on her answering machine, the expression in her voice. He considered standing there until she came home, no matter how long it took, but he grew tired and walked back through the silent neighborhood. When he came in his front door, he thought he caught a glimpse of Delia in the corner of the dining room.

That night his deceased wife came. She sat on the bed next to him, smiling and shaking her head. Her voice was strident and familiar.

"Porter, you old fool. Calling a strange woman like that? It didn't take you long, now, did it?" He tried to speak, but she put her fingers on his lips to quiet him. He wanted to protest that he had been totally faithful to her. Now he was never quite sure she believed that when she was alive. She had gone so quickly, and there were so many things he hadn't said to her. He was unable to speak and could only look up at her, her blond hair, her gray eyes.

She appeared more solid than he had expected, and younger than she was when she died. He wanted to know what he had done that needed forgiveness when he was in New Orleans, who Cody D. was, what was the name of that fabric softener that made his clothes smell like pine needles. Delia just smiled in her cautious way, shaking her head back and forth. She called him an old fool a few more times before her image faded.

Before sunrise the next morning, unable to sleep any longer, Porter walked the quiet streets under a smoky gray sky as he tried to remember his wife's ghostly visit the night before—the soft whiteness of her skin and the sheen of her hair and somber eyes, the timbre in her voice. Somewhere a rooster crowed. A dog barked. Rectangles of golden light appeared in a few of the houses as early risers switched on lamps. Porter walked trance-like and he almost tripped over something. When he looked down, he saw it was a flattened box of fabric softener sheets. Piney Fresh, the Scent of Wyoming in Your Clothes. He whispered the words Piney Fresh, hoping it would help him remember the brand name next time he went shopping.

By the time he got to her house, Annabel Embraces the Day was doing her nude sun salutation, and he cleared his throat loudly as he passed her fence. She didn't seem to flinch. Porter vowed for the twenty-ninth time in his life to give up cigarettes. He reminded himself to pick up ice cream on the way home, and started to think about where he might take Annabel Embraces the Day on their first date.

The Tub

They didn't say; "Don't use the tub." The Greens, who had hired Pam to be their pet sitter for five days, had left early that morning and Pam showed up around ten to take care of their golden lab and five cats. She would spend five days at their house. She had been there so many times that the job had become routine. No surprises. At least not yet.

The Tub stood in the large luxurious master bath, next to a glass-walled shower. Pam had always used the small guest bathroom. But this particular night she wanted a bath. In The Tub.

The sun was down and the house silent. All the cats in, as far as she could tell. Since they all kind of looked alike and were never in the same place at the same time, Pam had to trust that they all made it inside before she locked up for the night. The Tub, filled with hot water and a very generous amount of bubble bath oil, looked inviting. She lit a scented candle, which filled the damp air with the aroma of lilacs. The Tub, a very expensive, very new Jacuzzi bathtub, sat in an alcove next to a large window. Behind The Tub a marble shelf held a silver tray holding expensive bath products—creams and lotions and oils from France. The marble shelf extended across the whole edge of The Tub.

Tired from a long hot day of feeding five cats, cleaning out several cat boxes, walking the big golden lab three times, etc, etc, and continually taking couch pillows away from him, Pam lowered herself into the steamy water and leaned back, letting herself breathe deeply. Slowly, she could feel her tense muscles relaxing, her lungs opening and her breaths deepening. Different cats and the big dog walked by the open bathroom door that looked out into the hallway, which had a glass wall to the outside back patio. She could see the gray flagstone and lush plantings. She was in heaven—away from home and her usual responsibilities. Pet-sitting afforded Pam days and sometimes weeks in another world—luxurious homes with perks like swimming pools, beautiful gardens, hot tubs and Jacuzzis. All she had to do was give the animals lots of attention and leave the place as clean as she found it. Not a difficult task.

The warm water surrounded her body and she was starting to feel drowsy. Then she remembered the jets, strategically placed to send strong currents of water where most people need it—lower back, soles of the feet, hips, shoulders. With her right hand she felt for a button to turn on the jets. It took a while, but eventually she found the round flat switch and pushed. Underneath The Tub, Pam heard a rumbling noise and in a few seconds hot water came rushing out of the jets, causing all the water in the tub to swirl and bubble. It was so relaxing that she closed her eyes and dozed for what seemed like just a few moments. In a kind of altered state, Pam imagined she was in a pond of warm water, surrounded by lush jungle.

When she opened her eyes she noticed that the jets had churned the water so much that The Tub had filled with rich creamy foam. Pam felt like she was floating in whipped cream and as she lifted her arms out of the water, they seemed to be coated in iridescent puffs of snow. Soon the bubbles filled the entire alcove around The Tub. Pam casually tried to find the switch to turn off the jets but was unsuccessful. She watched the mountain of frothing bubbles grow around her and realized it was time to do something. Really.

The bubbles, now as high as her head, entirely filled the alcove and she watched them cascade close to the top of the marble edge of the bathtub, about to roll over onto the floor. She knew the switch was somewhere near her right knee and kept telling herself not to panic, that it would all be fine, but apprehension filled her stomach as she continued to search unsuccessfully for the switch.

Damn, she thought, if I weren't sitting here almost drowning in white foam I would be laughing hysterically watching someone else do this. Pam's body was so slippery from all the soap that she was afraid if she tried to get out of The Tub she would slip and break something and then what would she do? Crawl through the bubbles to the nearest phone and call 911? Does one call 911 for this kind of emergency? Perhaps she could throw on some clothes and scuttle to the neighbors—none of which she knew and all of whom lived quite far away. Then the Greens would find out and probably never ask her to pet sit again. She felt like a character in a Woody Allen movie, realizing it was up to her to figure this out. Cody, the big lab, came into the bathroom and watched all this with great interest. He had his red ball in his mouth.

Pam resumed her search for the turn-off switch as the foam frothed into huge peaks, which had now attached themselves to the screen of the open window above The Tub. She imagined the headlines: "Pet Sitter Dies in Tragic Jacuzzi Accident." There would be a photograph of the deadly Jacuzzi. Maybe a photo of Pam. And some smaller headline about how the family returned from a camping trip to find the house filled with lilac-scented foam, the pets unfed and no pet sitter in sight. The story would go on to state that the unfortunate pet sitter was found dead under a ton of suds. Death by asphyxiation. Oh God, don't let me die like this, she thought. Not now. She was leaving in two weeks to see her mother in Ohio. The shock would kill her. After all, she's eighty-three and already on shaky ground. And Pam's kids—how embarrassing to have their mother die this way. A victim of Jacuzzi forgetfulness.

Determined to find the button Pam slid her hand back and forth, which she had already done at least 100 times. Then, for the hell of it, she moved her hand higher up the side of the tub. Jackpot! She found the button, pushed it, and the rumbling and swishing stopped. Hallelujah! It still didn't seem safe to get out. She was too slippery and the foam too high to even see the edge of The Tub. She managed to pull up the plug and slowly the water drained while the suds remained. She didn't care. She had saved the day. With fresh water, Pam eventually removed the layer of slippery soap that covered her entire body.

During this whole process, she babbled away at the dog, who occasionally wandered in and then out of the bathroom. "What the hell was I thinking?" she asked him, as if the big yellow lab would explain it all to her. "Yes, yes, I know you're hungry, Cody. Hey, gimme a break already." Cody had now brought one of his toys into the bathroom and seemed to expect Pam to throw it for him to retrieve. He just looked at Pam, with what seemed like great amusement, cocking his head from side to side. Pam could hear his tail thumping against the marble floor. He wanted his nightly biscuit.

Baby Graves

Why I Hang Out with Crash

Baby Graves... who the hell is that? I don't know a Graves family that has a baby, but then, being new in town there are a lot of people I don't know yet.

"Do I know this Baby Graves?" I ask as we hustle up Canal Street.

"What?"

"Well, I thought maybe it's someone I know but don't know their name. Know what I mean? My dad called me Baby Ree until I was about seven, but everyone else called me Reola."

"What are you talking about?" His name is Charles, but everyone calls him Crash. His red hair looks like bumps and lumps. Crash lives across the street and he watched me from his front porch for three weeks before he even said hi.

What a creep, I thought. Crash the Goon. Crash the Smash. I hang out with him now only because I don't know anyone else to hang out with. I figure when school starts in a few weeks I'll make friends with the cool kids and Crash will be a thing of the past. I will say something like: "Well, yeah, I used to kinda be friends with him, but just in the beginning when I first moved here. Yeah, I know he's a crudball, but I was kinda desperate." And they will all smile and nod their heads—forgive me for hanging out with a creep because they know how cool I really am.

Crash walks fast, like in a walking race. I have to practically run to keep up with him. His legs are about three feet longer than mine. "Hey, slow down!" I yell. He is so far up the block that he doesn't even hear me. I feel sweat creeping down the sides of my pink sleeveless blouse. Damn!

"Hey, speak to me, Dumbo. Who is this Baby Graves person?" It sounds like an old blues singer. Crash just looks at me with his watery green eyes, blinking and making a strange face. He grabs my hand and pulls me across the street. God, I don't want anyone in town to see me holding his hand. What will people think? I snatch my hand away and Crash doesn't even seem to notice. He is busy pointing to the top of the hill, to a place where there aren't any buildings, just a few trees and lots of grass. Suddenly I realize it's the cemetery.

"The cemetery? Why the cemetery?"

"Hey, stupid, where else will you find baby graves?

Mom in a Box

Once my dad took me to a cemetery to see my grandma's grave. It's in Montana or Missouri or someplace with an M and we had to drive a long time to get there. It's just a flat rock, her grave. No big deal. I was too little to read, but it must have said her name and some dates. There were lots of other big flat rocks standing around and my dad told me they are the graves of all the people that are dead.

"Grandma, you in there?" I shouted into the grass. My dad said not to be a smartass and jerked my arm. For a long time I thought cemeteries are places where dead people live. Now I know that they are places to bury dead bodies and that the people who have their bodies in the ground are really up in heaven. Or someplace like heaven.

My mom doesn't have a grave we can visit. They had her cremated and shoved in a box. My dad has two pictures of her—one in a red dress holding a bottle of beer in her right hand. The other picture is of her standing sideways with me inside her belly. Her hands are underneath her huge stomach (me), and she's looking back over her shoulder laughing. She's very pretty in these pictures. When I was little I wondered how all of her could fit into a small box. That's before I understood about cremation.

"Look. Over there. Baby Graves." Crash stands behind me, kind of nudging me forward. On the top of a small hill I can see a white statue of a lamb and some more grey statues of angels and a baby Jesus. All across the grass are flat markers, like stepping stones. Something in my stomach squeezes and I back into Crash's body. "Hey," he says quietly. His voice is low and whispery. "Come on. Don't be afraid. I'm right here." He says this like he's my dad, which I hate. I stomp up the hill and step on those graves, like I'm crossing a creek on rocks. I look at Crash and he just shakes his head from side to side, like I am stupid or something. Like I'm a dog that doesn't know better.

"You know, that's really not the way to do it, Reola. It's kinda disrespectful." Damn, I hate that word. I hear it a lot these days, since everything I do is disrespectful, according to someone who is older than me. Crash is two years older. Fourteen. I sigh the way I see ladies do in the movies. I know I'm supposed to say I'm sorry or something like that. I don't.

Rule Number One... Ask a Lot of Questions

"Hey, Ree. Where did you and Crash go? I saw you two walking up the street a few hours ago." My Aunt Sadie is putting mashed potatoes on the table. The potatoes look like fluffy clouds sitting in the cracked green bowl.

Her face is red from cooking, greasy smudges all over her apron. I don't want to answer the question and run to the kitchen to bring out a plate of green beans. Sadie the Lady—that's what we call her, my dad and me. Aunt Sadie cooks what my dad calls "he-man food." Lots of potatoes and meatloaf and macaroni and cheese and stuff like beets and green beans and peas and carrots. There's lots of butter and the salt is so heavy it burns your throat sometimes. My dad is in heaven.

"Ree, your aunt asked you a question. And, as a matter of fact, I'm kinda curious myself. Where did you go with that Crash character?" I stuff my mouth with a load of beans mixed with potatoes and hold up my pointing finger to signal for him to wait a minute while I chew. My dad's afraid of me choking, so he never asks me a question or yells at me when I have food in my mouth. I chew for a long time, making sure every morsel has turned into something watery and has no more taste. When I think no one is looking I shove in another ton of meatloaf dipped in more potatoes. My dad doesn't seem to notice. He's busy scraping his potatoes into a small pile on the side of his plate. Sadie winks at me. She knows I'm avoiding something. Women's Intuition.

After dessert my dad asks the same question again, now that there's nothing in my mouth that I can choke on. "So tell us, honey. What did you and Crash do today? Where were you going?" Damn, I don't want them to know. Visiting Baby Graves just seems so... so... dumb.

"Aw, we were just takin' a walk, Dad. You know. Right foot, left foot, right foot, left foot. Like that. Nothin' special." He looks satisfied and opens the paper. Sometimes it seems that my dad doesn't listen to one thing I say. He asks a lot of questions but I can see his eyes turn to glass by the time I'm on my third word. He must have read a book on how to be a good dad. *Guidebooks for Single Fathers, or How to Act Like You Give a Shit When You Really Haven't Got a Clue How To Raise a Child and Are Doing It Only Because Your Wife Died.* Rule number one, Ask a Lot of Questions.

I Don't Want to Talk About It

Crash and I are visiting Baby Graves. I'm not so weirded out this time. I promise not to step on anyone's grave and tiptoe around them. Reading names and dates: *Our Beloved Mildred, Born June 16 1913, Died June 17 1913; Baby Tater 1926-1928, two years, five months and three days old.*

Some of the markers are nothing more than a slab of stone flat on the ground and you can't read anything. Some are short little headstones carved with lambs or crosses or flowers and words and dates and little sayings. *We held you in our arms but a moment. Now he is with the Angels. Gone to her Home in Heaven. Our Blessed One.* Reading these things makes me sad and embarrassed. It's like looking in someone's drawer and finding something they wouldn't want you to see.

Some of the names are weird—Sarah Joy, Agatha Beale, Stanton James La Crosse, Adelaide Somerville. I imagine dead babies in tiny caskets, wearing old-fashioned clothes. I imagine crying parents, lots of brothers and sisters, everyone in black. Weeping.

"Do babies get cremated?" I ask Crash. I don't know if he knows what cremated means, but I'm prepared to explain it to him if he doesn't. He just pops a piece of Juicy Fruit in his mouth and chews for a long time. I can smell sweet gum each time he breathes out. His eyes look around like he's checking to see if anyone's listening.

"Cremated? You mean like, when you like, burn someone up?" I nod my head yes. He hums to let me know he is still thinking about it. A bunch of little yellow birds all fly out of a maple tree and swirl around like waves in the air until they find another tree to disappear into. I can tell Crash doesn't know the answer to this one, but I'm kinda surprised he even knows what cremated is.

"My mom was cremated. A long time ago when she died." When I say this it makes me feel special, like I am some kind of rare bird or something. Crash's eyes get real big, like a surprise.

"You shittin' me?"

"No, she was. A long time ago, when I was born. I never knew her, but my dad kept her ashes in a box until I was about five."

"What happened?"

"Well, we were movin' around too much and the box kept gettin' scratched and bumped and my dad said that Mom never liked moving too much, so we decided to leave her."

"What do you mean? You just left the box somewhere?"

"No. It's not like that. It was different. I don't want to talk about it."

Everything was Soft With Mom

When I shook it, it sounded like a soft rattle, like a rattle for a tiny baby. More noise than ashes should make, like there were some big pieces in there. Pieces of what? Daddy told me it is my mom, but I was too young to understand how a Mom could fit in such a small box and be so quiet when you shook her like that. He said never mind and we drove to a lake. I asked if Mom liked this lake and he said that she never saw this lake but that she liked lakes in general and will be happy here. I thought he was talking about a city named General and asked him: "Where is General?" He told me not to be a smartass.

It was a long drive. We had a map to show us how to get there. Daddy said Emerald Mirror Lake will be a good place because Mom liked emeralds and was always looking in the mirror. The sky was very gray and I was afraid it was going to rain and I thought that Mom wouldn't want to finally get out of the box on a rainy day. I didn't say anything because my dad seemed to know what he was doing.

A man rented us a rowboat and Dad had the box hidden in a big pack he was carrying. He said shh to me a lot, which meant don't open your mouth. He acted all cheerful with the man, talking about taking his little girl out on a boat for the first time. I saw black clouds coming together in the sky. Daddy didn't seem to notice. He just rowed until we were far away from the shore. I didn't say anything at all, just sat and watched him looking at the box, looking at the water, scratching his face.

I don't know what I thought was in the box. Daddy has said over and over "it's ashes, just ashes" but somehow I thought the ashes would look like my Mom. I only knew her from some pictures we have— round face, short hair, big black eyes, lots of very white teeth. I thought of her as always smiling, just like in the pictures. The ashes were gray, soft like dust. He turned the box upside down and they slid out until they hit the wind and blew around my head like smoke—getting dust on my skin. Some of the pieces hit the water and made this noise— pitpitpitpit.

Mom, all over my bluejeans, on my fingertips. Everything was soft with Mom and I breathed her into my nose and pressed her into my arms and around and around on the palms of my hands, making them slick and slidey with Mom. Mom all around me. And in the distance was thunder and a cold wind slapped against me. My dad had Mom on his eyelashes and across the top of his head.

He's a Smartass, That Crash

Baby Bingham; Our Precious Cecil; Statucci Twins Franceso and Francesca, Three days on this Earth; Eternally with Our Lord in Heaven; Our Beloved Baby Boy; The Baby.

Some are polished and shiny, carved with vines or trumpets or funny looking crosses. Some of the graves have six pointed stars. Crash calls them the Baby Jew Graves. He said that dead Jew babies are buried naked and that nobody is allowed to see them after they're dead, except a special kind of priest that wears his hair funny and long black coats. When I ask him why, he pretends not to hear me and I know he doesn't know why and is embarrassed to say it.

My Aunt Sadie told me that Crash got his name when he was a little kid. She doesn't remember how old he was, but he was riding his tricycle and crashed into a brick wall. He got a big old bloody nose and broke something else. She can't remember what exactly he broke, but ever since then his family called him Crash. She told me this one time when she was giving me a Toni Home Permanent out on the back porch. It made my hair all crinkly and I wanted to kick her but I restrained myself (restrain is my dad's word for not doing what you really want to do). I restrain a lot around Aunt Sadie.

I find a little circle of four baby graves. These markers look different from the others. Each is a rectangle, with a different design. One has four butterflies, one in each corner. Another one, under the shade of an old tree, has nothing but tiny round circles attached to each other, like a chain that you make out of construction paper at Christmas. One has the outline of a hand, nothing else, in the middle of the stone. The fourth one has a date inside a circle. 1954.

Crash is on the other side of the tree yelling out dates to me. We're looking for the oldest grave. "Hey, here's a 1832 and another 1857." He is keeping a list of all the dates. It's research, he says. I guess just looking at the Baby Graves isn't enough. He'll probably write a report about it for class or something.

"Come here. Look at these." Crash is like a bad dog and never comes the first two times you call him. After the third command, he comes over and looks over my shoulder. "Yeah?"

"Well, look at these. Why are they all together and why don't they have any names and just one has a date?" Crash snorts and looks like he wants to pick his nose, except I'm standing right next to him.

"Hell, I've seem 'em lots of times. But if they don't have a date, they can't be part of the research."

"You mean they don't count?" I'm angry. Why don't these babies count I want to know.

"Because they aren't dated. Except that one. So, if it'll make you happy that one'll be part of the research. Okay, young lady?" He heard my dad yelling young lady at me one night when we were having a fight. He's a smartass, that Crash.

Big and Round Like a Light Bulb

"Reola, where do you and Crash go?" Aunt Sadie's head is looking down at her sewing, but her eyes are pointed up at me. She's so weird.

"Don't tell anyone. Okay? I know he's a stupid jerk head, but there just isn't anyone in the neighborhood I can hang out with. When school starts I'll meet all the cool girls and then Crash will be his-tor-eee."

"I know." But she can't really know. My Aunt Sadie's too square to understand about being cool and the danger of being seen hanging out with a creep like Crash. She wears clunky shoes and really ugly blouses that tie into a big bow under her neck. She isn't pretty like my mom. She's not even related to my mom. She's just my dad's sister. Her arms are flabby on the upper part and her butt is big and round like a light bulb. When we go shopping I see men looking at her butt. I know what they are thinking, "Hey, lookit that huuuuuge butt. I wouldn't want that huuuuuge butt sittin' in my lap." And all those smiles they give her. What's that about?

"I was just wondering where you two go off to every day. Just curious. It's good for Crash to have a friend. He's a nice kid but kinda lonely. He's an only child just like you."

How did she know we went off every day? She's supposed to be working down at the insurance office on Market Street, right in the middle of town. Some days I walk into town and I can see her through the big smudgy window, punching the keys on a typewriter, her light bulb butt on that little chair. She has a picture of JFK on her desk, framed, like he's her husband or something. And another one of Jackie and John John and Caroline squinting in the sun. Sadie's kinda creepy, but my dad likes her. She's his sister, so what do you expect?

"Uh, we uh, go places. Yeah, just places."

"What kinda places, Ree?" Shit, does she have to know everything?

"Uh, I don't know. I can't remember. We just hang out around the neighborhood." Sadie makes this humphing noise, like "I give up." I pretend that I have to pee and dawdle in the bathroom for a long time. By the time I come down, she's making dinner, singing to some dopey song on the radio.

Making Biscuits

Longxin Wu, 1921-1926 (stand-up marker with a carving of a rabbit); Bernard Zywynsky, Our Precious Baby, 1959; Anapoura, Sabinya and Reza, Mother and Child, July 27 1937; Baby Black; Baby Loungue; Our Little Angel, 1898-1900; Forever in our Hearts; Bruce, 1920-1923.

Looking at all these baby graves makes me kinda sad. So many babies. What if they didn't die? Would the town be much, much bigger? I find babies born the same year as me (1957). They could have been my friends, maybe even live on the same street as my dad and me and Aunt Sadie.

Aunt Sadie is making biscuits and I'm helping, stirring and sifting and pouring in milk.

"Hey, Aunt Sadie. You ever been married?"

"Uh huh. Long time ago. Before you were born."

"You divorced?" She has flour wiped across her face and I scrub at my face because I don't want to look stupid like that.

"Yeah, you might say." I wait. She doesn't say anything more.

"Oh. You knew my mom?"

"Uh huh. A bit, I knew her. We lived far apart, but I met her a few times. The last time I saw her she had you in her tummy." Well, what do you know. She knew me before I was me. "Your mom was a sweet one. Kinda innocent. I liked her pretty much. She sure was excited about you coming into the world." Aunt Sadie is smiling in her mouth but her eyes look kinda sad.

"You ever have any kids, Aunt Sadie?"

"Uh huh."

"Where are they?" Aunt Sadie never talks about her kids. Maybe they had a big fight or something.

"Oh honey, they're not here anymore." Aunt Sadie is touching my hand and it makes me feel kinda creepy, like I'm supposed to say something to make her feel better.

"OK. I was just curious." I don't like doing it, but I get up and go up to my room and sit on the bed real quiet so the springs don't squeak so maybe Aunt Sadie will forget the whole thing. Like I never asked. I think I know what she means.

At dinner everyone is kinda quiet, but the biscuits are sweet and fluffy.

She Never Had No Luck. Never

One night I ask my dad about Aunt Sadie's kids. "Oh honey. She had some bad luck. I don't think you want to know about it."

"Yeah, I wanna know. I'm not a little kid anymore. You can tell me." My dad hates that I'm growing up. I can tell. He sometimes calls me Baby Ree behind my back, when he's talking to Aunt Sadie.

"Honey, some people just come into the world for troubles. Your Aunt Sadie's one of them. She never had no luck. Never."

"What happened?"

"Well, first she married that Pizzoli."

"What's a Pizzoli?"

"He was your uncle."

"Uncle Pizzoli?"

"Uncle Mario. Mario Pizzoli, the little shithead punk. Pop warned her, but she had the hots for him. No one could stop her from runnin' away with him."

I can see him—short with black curly hair and huge muscles. A shithead punk.

"He got big muscles and black hair, Dad?"

"Who, Pizzoli? Nah, he was a short skinny thing. Sadie musta outweighed him by thirty pounds. He was nothin' but trouble and broke Sadie's heart."

I wonder how a short skinny guy could break someone's heart, but I don't say anything 'cause I know my dad. Once he gets started, he'll tell you the whole story. Beginning to end. Just like that.

"Uncle Mario was a drunk and he got in trouble with the law. Uncle Mario played around." I don't think it means going to the playground to play on the swings. I think it has something to do with sex. (I know all about sex). "He owed a bunch of people in town a lot of money." I keep thinking about Aunt Sadie with her flabby upper arms, outweighing Uncle Mario by thirty pounds. "He was just a no gooder."

"But what about Sadie?"

"Well, she pretended everything was okay. She never had no luck, that Sadie. Then the kids started comin'. One right after the other, and each one lived just a few days or a few weeks. Something genetic, but it must have come from the Pizzolis. We never had nothin' like that in our family. Those damn Pizzoli's broke Sadie's heart." My dad has a long face, so I wait for him to say more. "And then the bastard just takes off and no one ever hears from him again."

My dad looks kinda upset, so I bring him a lemonade. We're on the front porch and the light's on in Crash's room across the street. Probably writing his report on Baby Graves. Aunt Sadie's playing poker with the girls tonight. I wonder if they know about Pizzoli and the babies. I don't even know how many there were. Dad doesn't look like talking anymore. But there's one thing I have to know.

"Dad. Those babies. Are they buried somewhere?"

"I don't know, honey. I wasn't here when it happened. I was away in the army. We weren't close then. I only heard about it through the family." He yawns and belches.

We'll See About That

Crash is spending a lot of time on his research. His oldest Baby Grave was born in 1782 and died in 1783. *Our Precious Dolores, one year old.* You can hardly read the words and have to get real close to see it. The stone is cracked and peeling. We put a piece of white paper over the words and rubbed a black crayon. That's how we know what it says. Crash thinks the name is Felores, but I told him that's a stupid name. It must be Delores. Whoever heard of a Felores?

Since my dad and I had our "little talk" (Honey, I don't think you should tell Sadie about our little talk. Okay?) Aunt Sadie is different. I don't know what it is. She isn't so weird or clunky. Maybe she wants to be like my mom or something. I try to be nice to her. She wanted to sew me some new school clothes. I wanted clothes from Sears, but I said she could sew me three things. Only three. She kinda smiled at that. She went out and bought patterns and material. It's not the coolest, but I can wear it when I hang out at home. I almost want to make her feel good. No one ever wanted to sew me clothes. My dad can't even remember what grade I'm in.

School starts in three days. I don't know if Crash and I will be hanging out together anymore, but I'm thinking about still visiting the Baby Graves. I never see anyone else up there visiting them. A few days ago I stole flowers from some old man's garden and put them on top of those four markers that have no names on them. Weird. It made me feel good.

Boy, am I ready to meet the cool girls. There just isn't anyone good in this neighborhood. Dad says we're settling in at Aunt Sadie's. I guess he means we'll stay for a while. It's OK by me. Sadie thinks she's going to take me to school the first day. We'll see about that.

I Don't GOT ONE

Mr. Kesselman is the principal at my new school. He's very short and fat and has a lisp. What a creep. The first day of school I walk into the office. Thomas Jefferson Junior High. Yuck, what a stupid name for a school. Why do they always name schools after dead old guys? My old school was Picket Elementary because it was on Picket Street. Now that makes sense, but this Thomas Jefferson guy?

"May I help you young lady?" (That stupid young lady thing again). Mr. Kesselman's smells like Vicks VapoRub.

"I'm new in town and today's the first day of school. Can I come to this school?"

"Of course, young lady. But you should have brought your mother with you to fill out some paperwork." Damn, the mother thing again.

"I don't GOT ONE"

"I'm sorry? You don't have one?" Kesselman's chewing on a pencil and looking at his watch.

"A mother. I don't GOT ONE."

"How about your father?"

"He's at work. Like you." Now Kesselman's really frustrated.

"Well, dear, you will have to bring an adult with you to register you at this school. Isn't there anyone?"

"Sadie. She's my aunt. But I have to go get her. She works too."

I go into town to get Aunt Sadie. All she says is "I told you." We have to sit in Kesselman's office and he's asking her a lot of questions and keeps calling me "your daughter." After three times Sadie stops reminding him that I'm only her niece. Why bother? He doesn't get it. He keeps calling me Rowena instead of Reola.

I had to miss all of home room because we had lots of paperwork to fill out. Fine by me. The school secretary walks me to the auditorium where Mr. K. is having some sort of stupid assembly. The band, which really stinks, is just finishing the song about the pocket's red pear. I take a seat in the back row.

Mr. K. reads a list of names of all the new students in the school. My stomach starts to feel funny, but when he gets to the end of the B's without saying my name and starts with the C's, I kind of relax. Each new kid has to go to the front of the auditorium and stand facing everyone else. God, this is dumb.

After he says the last two names (Penny Waddle and Darius Zooner), he says my name. Well, kinda. Instead of Reola Bones, he says Rowena Banes. I know he means me. Everyone is real quiet, looking around for this Rowena Banes person. Kesselman spies me sitting in the back and makes a motion with his hands for me to come up. His fingers are open wide, like a baseball glove and he's making big circles, like he's pulling in a fish or something. He thinks this is funny and some of the kids laugh. Damn, I gotta go up there. My knees are shaking like anything. I keep my head straight, but move my eyes back and forth. This makes me look cool as a cucumber, like I'm not interested in anything.

I'm looking for the cool girls. I see girls that look like me— kinda dopey with bad hair and dumb clothes. There's lots of blond girls. They must be the cool ones. Maybe no one here knows that I used to hang out with Crash.

Maybe There's Hope for Me One Day

Aunt Sadie's cooking up a storm for Thanksgiving. Some of her poker girls are coming over for dinner. All they do is laugh and gossip and drink highballs, but a couple of them are okay. The turkey is so gross looking, all white and goose bumpy, that I had to leave the house.

"Hey Ree, honey. Don't forget we have biscuits to make. Come back in about an hour. Okay?" Sadie now calls me honey a lot. God, she's so motherly I can hardly stand it. I decide to go see the Baby Graves again. There are two new ones: *June 11, 1969 (*no name*); Melinda, our Precious Daughter, August 14, 1969.*

I wonder if Crash knows about these new graves. I never see him in the cemetery anymore. I guess he's just so busy at high school. I wonder if he ever wrote that paper after all the research we did last summer.

I walk over to the four graves that are all in a circle. I visit them a lot. Sometimes I steal some flowers from someone's yard and put them in the middle of the circle.

Dad got a new job down at some factory that makes tractors. That means we'll be staying here for a while. He says at least till the end of the school year. Aunt Sadie's spending a lot of time sewing stuff like curtains and nightgowns and skirts for me. I hate them, but my dad says I should be grateful and if I say anything mean to her he'll hit me or something. I don't know what the "or something" could be, so I act nice.

I have new friends from school. Most of them are dopey like me but some are blond. They're the cool ones. No one mentions Crash's name so I guess no one knows we used to hang out and I don't have to make excuses.

~ ~ ~

I think Crash has a girlfriend. I see them walking down the street sometimes. She's actually kinda pretty and she laughs a lot. I don't remember Crash being funny. Once I saw them kiss, just a little peck-peck on the lips. But you know, if Crash can find someone to kiss and laugh with, maybe that means there's hope for me someday.

Remembering Maggie

Elliot remembers meeting Maggie in the Amsterdam train station, waiting for the train to take them to Rome. He had been traveling alone for several weeks, a pseudo hippie in jeans and a ripped leather jacket, growing a beard and his hair in an attempt to create a new persona. He was, actually, a fairly conservative engineering student at the University of Pittsburgh, acting on a whim. Having taken the summer off to work in the steel mills, he made a decision that was quite unlike him. With a few thousand dollars in his bank account, he decided to do something totally irrational and fly to Europe rather than returning to classes in September. It was Thanksgiving and he was feeling alone and blue that particular day. He longed for turkey and cranberries and family arguments across a well-set dinner table.

Maggie sat on a bench not far from him, her suitcase squeezed between her legs as if she expected someone, at any moment, to attempt to snatch it away from her. Nervous, timid and watchful, twenty years old, out of England alone for the first time. She sat stiffly, reading a book and playing with her hair. He expected her to slip her thumb into her mouth and start sucking any minute. She told him she was from London, on her way to Rome to visit her aunt. He offered her a cigarette. They talked about the book she was reading. Proust. He hid his Ian Flemming in a pocket of his backpack and asked her if she would like to sit with him on the train. She nodded her head eagerly up and down as if his invitation had released a huge burden for her.

139

They ended up with their own musty compartment—second class, smoking. Sitting across from each other, they looked out the window, watched the passing scenery and ate strong cheese and crumbly biscuits she had brought for the trip. He, the "seasoned" traveler, felt somehow responsible for her, and imagined a phone call she would make to her parents when she got to Rome, praising the kindness of an American stranger—a hippie who ended up being quite polite, and yes, he was even clean. He told her he was twenty-seven and she believed him. He was twenty-two at the time.

They smoked cigarettes and sucked on lemon drops from a round flat tin as the train crossed Germany. She wore a lot of brown. Brown loafers, brown skirt, a brown wool sweater. She looked like a character out of a British play, discerning and self contained. Even her backpack was brown and sensible. Somewhere, he has a photograph of her, in her British clothes with her British haircut —blunt and short. Her white skin seemed untouched by the sun. Maggie mentioned that the last time she saw any real sun had been three years earlier when her father took her on holiday to Italy. He loved it when she referred to anything that closely resembled a vacation as a "holiday," as if her life was so dreary that she needed to make any break from the ordinary seem somehow festive. To him, holiday meant fireworks and hot dogs and cotton candy. To her it meant getting on the train and going somewhere other than the place you live. He was charmed by what he assumed to be her narrow exposure to the exotic, to color, to sunshine.

He now recalls that later that evening they had sex. Elliot can't remember who initiated it, no memory of actually being attracted to her. She seemed so naive and childlike, like a younger cousin or a friend's sister—someone he would never consider having sex with. Even when he looks at the few snapshots he took, she seems waif-like and stiff, a girl clothed in dull colors with knobby knees and glasses.

They never really got undressed, although Maggie did take off a few articles of clothing. She insisted on wearing her scratchy wool skirt and brown knee socks. "In case someone breaks in," she claimed, as if a stranger walking in would look at them and say how delightful it was to see two young people fucking while partially clothed, and thank God that girl had the decency to keep on her good woolen skirt. (But your Honor, I did keep my skirt on. That counts for something, now, doesn't it?) At Maggie's suggestion, he kept on his sweater and socks. She insisted that they open the window and the compartment was ice cold. The train chugged through the Alps and moved forward in jerks, jolting the car back and forth as the track curved through the steep mountain passes. Keeping their balance was difficult.

He remembers very little about the sex itself, except that the whole thing was terribly awkward. She kept whispering a phrase over and over—a line from the Beatles' song Strawberry Fields Forever. "Let me take you down." Maggie repeated those words like a mantra, under her breath, against the side of his neck, her words damp and soft, subdued and gentle. She was, he remembers, without passion, most likely without experience. She seemed almost disconnected from her body, as if in a trance state.

In his memory, he felt like an animal, devouring the moment for his own pleasure. He heard his breath filling the frigid compartment, heard himself groaning and grunting—a sound that, with age and experience, he eventually learned to tone down into a more appropriate, human noise. No discussion of birth control or sexually transmitted diseases occurred. Ah, the oblivion of the seventies when we were all too willing to follow our urges without any thought of consequences. It seemed that he labored over her longer than usual. Perhaps it was the circumstances—the locked compartment door, the possible intrusion of a conductor checking passports or tickets. Her scratchy skirt wasn't helping matters either. Having an allergy to wool, he felt a rash blossoming with each thrust. Maggie, on the other hand, simply lay there with her legs opened, repeating her mantra. "Let me take you down." For all he knew, she might have been fantasizing that she was making it with John or Paul or George or even Ringo. Hard to tell, and he sensed that it was a sacred thing that he dare not mention.

As they struggled into their clothes he told Maggie that he thought it fortuitous that no one came into their compartment while they were "at it." Maggie said that it was destiny rather than fortune. He was an atheist, blubbering on about free choice and the kindness of luck. He argued that there was no such thing as fate, that life was merely a string of random events. The more passionately she argued, the more British she sounded and the more animated she became. "But Elliot, there are too many synchronicities in the universe to be merely random, now aren't there" (said as a statement rather than a question), her sallow cheeks becoming blotchy and pink with passion seemed to be reserved only for philosophical discourse.

When they went out into the corridor to stretch their legs, he imagined he was in one of those foreign films where women smoke like men and men lean out of train windows. He wanted to hear a concertina playing French ballads over the rhythmic sound of iron wheels clattering along tracks. He felt emptied and self-satisfied. Eventually they returned to their compartment, stretching out on seats opposite each other, and slept until the sun rose. In the morning they talked little, as if what had occurred just a few hours earlier had been some kind of strange dream. As if they had just met for the first time, each reluctant to say too much.

The train let them off in Rome, and he made sure she knew where to go. He helped direct her as she seemed a bit confused and, suddenly, very young.

He never saw Maggie again. He said goodbye as she walked off arm-in-arm with her aunt, getting into a taxi. During the month he was in Rome he looked for her on the street, regretting that they hadn't made plans to meet each other. He tried to find a book by Proust in English, imagining that they would run into each other one day in an espresso bar and have a wonderful conversation about the book. He fantasized that she had been a virgin. That he was Maggie's ideal. The exotic hippie who introduced her to wild American passion. This fantasy remained for years.

Of course, looking back years later, Elliot would hope that she would never again have to endure a lover as selfish and oafish as he had been at the time. He saw the whole incident as a rash, pathetic act. He imagined her sitting in a circle of women sharing their sexual histories, that Maggie had told them about the animal noises and total lack of consideration for her feelings. He cringed to think that his name might become a catch-phrase for disappointing sexual experiences. All a woman had to say was "he's such an Elliot" and the others would laugh, knowingly. He thought of all the things he would have done differently. But then, perhaps she was correct, that it was destiny that he, all these years later, was left feeling like he had started a sentence and left it dangling on the tip of his tongue.

Elliot's life now takes him to London a few times a year and occasionally he finds himself looking for Maggie. He is not sure he would recognize her. They are both thirty years older and he has lost most of his hair, his jeans and the ripped leather jacket. He has lost most of his arrogance. It's been hammered down by life and loss and more mistakes than he cares to mention. Still, he looks into shop windows and searches the faces of women his age in pubs and restaurants. He doesn't know what it would be like for him to actually find Maggie standing on a street corner. He imagines her still dressed in brown with her severe clipped hair and pale skin, still referring to any change in her schedule as a "holiday." And then he considers that she probably remembers him as the awkward arrogant jerk he was thirty years ago, or worse yet, that she has totally forgotten him. And suddenly he is relieved that he has never run into her.

The End of the Journey

Surrendering to the hot steamy air and the echoing sounds of bare feet flapping across the marble floor, I sit naked on a stone bench, watching the sensuous beauty of women in this ancient structure. A high dome made of small round pieces of glass receives the late afternoon sun, shining down in rods of golden light, into a bee-hive of naked women and cascading water. Almost the end of my journey, a few weeks before I return to my real life.

The year is 1987. I am in Cağaloğlu Hamam, a Turkish bath in Istanbul. Across the street, the Grand Bazaar, the largest souk in Turkey, swarms with shoppers, lookers and pick pockets. Women in headscarves and long coats, even in the summer heat, carry baskets, going from vendor to vendor, buying small pieces of goat meat, a few dates for a special recipe, a bar of scented soap. Each item chosen carefully and with much bargaining. Dozens of alleys lead to rows and rows of men selling carpets, glazed tiles, brassware, copperware, hookas, jewelry, lamps. I have just bought myself an opal ring, flashing with fire. Close by, the Spice Bazaar sends up wafts of exotic fragrance. Captured by a scent, it leads me down a brick alleyway to the man selling saffron in bright golden threads. I am surrounded by clanging bells and loud bargaining in languages I don't understand.

The men in Turkey are respectful as they flirt outrageously. They ask me out for drinks, they have "special" rugs to show me, they practice their English with me. After three months of travelling across Western and Eastern Europe and now on the edge of Asia I am both frazzled and softened by the burning sun of a long summer. The bustling cities of Holland, Italy and France, the white sands of Croatia and the brilliant blue skies of the Greek islands have led me to this intensely exotic and beautiful city.

At the humum, I wait to be called for my turn. I pour brass bowls of warm water over my head. Each dousing sends shivers of pleasure down my spine. Water supplies in many of the places I passed through have been limited. Now, the echo of sloshing liquid fills the space. The air, steamy and incredibly humid, provides comfort in the warmth. All around a huge circular space women lounge, sit, walk back and forth. Some have towels around their heads. Young women, old women, middle-aged ones. Women of all color and size, naked and exposed. Some are gathered in groups, laughing together. Some, like me, sit alone beside open brass spigots of seemingly endless water.

She nods to me and presses her palm on the pedestal before her. I walk to her and she motions for me to sit. The stone is surprisingly warm. She tells me with her hands and her eyes and something in Turkish to lie on my stomach. I obey. I am here to submit to this experience, exhausted and dirty from travelling and weeks of two minute rinses, cold showers on Greek islands, cleaning myself with water collected in plastic bottles in areas where the water is turned off every afternoon until the next day. Unfamiliar toilets, dirty sheets and much dirtier trains and ferries and busses, not to mention a few donkeys. I offer my treasure trove of shmutz and dead skin to this woman with whom I have no common language.

Istanbul is a place I never imagined I would see. I had no itinerary for this trip. At fourty-two, I simply put on a backpack and took off for Europe. Exactly where I would end up was all a matter of chance. All I knew was that I was to fly into Amsterdam and out of Athens. My travels in between, up for grabs. A man I had met in Florence raved about Turkey. I kept it in the back of my mind and when I got to the island of Rhodes, with the coast of southern Turkey a few hours away by boat, I decided to spend the end of my journey trusting my internal compass. A kind of reward. For being courageous, trusting, adventurous. For many sleepless nights on trains and boats, not to mention a night spent sleeping on a sidewalk in Athens, watching rats the size of Dobermans circling the area. For learning smatterings of foreign languages. My intention was to follow my intuition and see where it took me.

She appears to be much older than me, although judging from the few women I have seen in the villages during my week long meander through the Turkish provinces, she could have been my own age. Large and muscled, she wears nothing but black panties, like all the other workers in the humum. Skin the color of a walnut shell, lustrous in the damp air. Full lips and kind eyes. She speaks only Turkish, but I understand what she is telling me. I fold my arms and lay my head down, eyes closed, anticipating her large hands squeezing and molding my muscles into something other than the iron shields they have become.

In my real life I am a masseuse and have had a private practice for almost twelve years. I learned to keep this fact a secret, especially when I got to Italy and travelled east. It wasn't worth the time it took to explain that not all women who do massage are prostitutes. No really, I reassured them, it's different in California. Ah yes. California. Where weirdness abounds.

A loofa scours my skin over and over. It isn't what I thought it would be and I try to stay relaxed. It feels harsh and pleasurable at the same time. I breathe deeply and allow my muscles to soften to her vigorous scrapings. Concentrating on the soles of my feet, scraping away months of travel dirt, she is scratching an itch deep inside my body. It fills me with pleasure. The harsh scrubber she uses seems to be polishing the entire backside of my body. It is both stimulating and relaxing. Between scrubs, she pours brass bowls of warm water over me.

When I flip over onto my back, she can tell my breasts are sensitive. When I put my hands up to protect them, she pulls them away and nods her head. She says something in Turkish and after that she avoids scrubbing that area. Either her scraping becomes gentler or I am simply trusting her more and more. As a masseuse, I know how important trust is during a massage. Nudeness and being touched by a stranger is a fragile combination. Working on someone's body is a privilege I have learned to be grateful for each time I do my work. Touch can release memories and emotions. It can be a healing experience. All I can do at this point is take deep breaths and hope to discharge some of the tension I have been carrying.

As she scrapes away weeks of accumulated dirt and dead skin, I can hear her humming against the background of sloshing water, womens' laugher and distant conversations. Her voice is deep and sonorous. Some of the workers sing as they work. The cacophony of sounds could lull me into sleep if I let it. Occasionally, she brings her face close to mine and says things like: "You okay, lady? You vedy vedy much dirt." She has dyed dark hair and large eyes the color of shiny black olives. She may have been beautiful as a younger woman. She is still quite lovely, although she has the look of one who has been through hard times. Maybe a bad marriage. Maybe money problems. Maybe she hates her job. She occasionally calls out to the other women. Perhaps she complains about me. "This dirty American…" Probably she's just talking about what she will make for dinner that night.

She motions for me to get up and follow her. My body is slow and loose. Walking feels a bit unsteady and she takes my hand the way a mother takes the hand of a small child who is first learning to walk. She sits on a chair and indicates that I am to sit facing away from her on a low stool, between her legs. I run my hands over my body. It feels slippery and clean and smooth. There is no more dead skin and I realize I am not as tan as I thought I was. She begins to wash my hair. Strong fingers massage my head. Small circles from her thumbs press and dig into my scalp. Slowly, my body relaxes and she pours something in my hair that smells of wax and honey. Her hands cradle my head as she washes my hair. I can hear suds, the sound of tiny bubbles crashing into each other, emitting a final gasp right before the tiniest tender "pop." She gently pulls my head back and carefully pours water over my hair, protecting my eyes with the palm of her hand pressed against my forehead to create of funnel as the water runs to the floor around me. She is accomplished at what she does and I imagine she has done this work, perhaps, all her life.

Something in my body lets go and I let myself melt against her strong thighs. Large hands begin to massage my neck and shoulders. Her touch is strong and confident, finding the places where my muscles have bunched together. The cause of headaches and difficulty falling asleep. My body surrenders more and I moan softly with pleasure. I sigh. She chuckles and says something in Turkish. I want this moment to never end. I take her hand and kiss it. She understands. She is pleased and leans down and smiles at me. Her teeth are straight and white, her lips full and the lines around her eyes are beautiful. "You like," she tells me, knowingly. I am delighted and nod. She laughs and hums a new song, occasionally sprinkling words into the notes. The melody is in a minor key, ancient and haunting, a love song I imagine. I am in heaven, captured in the pleasure of my now clean body. Wall sconces have been turned on, giving the room a golden luminosity that filters through the moist steamy air. I can smell incense.

When she is done, she takes a white towel from a hook on the wall, hands it to me and points to where I am to walk. She has made me happy and clean. I thank her over and over and then find my way to the small stone-walled cubicle where I left my clothes. There is a bed covered in white sheets and I lie down, wrapped in my towel. My breathing is deep, as if my lungs have been opened. I doze. When I wake up, the sun is setting. Istanbul at night is mysterious and exotic. I shiver in the cooling air and flag down a taxi. I feel clean and shiny, hungry for lamb and rice, succulent figs and olives. The setting sun, over the Bosphorus Strait, a golden apricot in a deep azure sky.

Author's Note

The other day I watched a documentary about Norah Ephron, who was quoted as saying: "Writers are cannibals." I found her words provocative. So of course, I decided to look inside and see if that rings true for me. And it does. I realize that I devour life that occurs around me. I watch the details. The crumbs that haven't been swept off the table before the beautiful vase of flowers is put down. The gestures people make that articulate much more than their words. The ways we communicate in spite of no shared lexicon. I have been this way since I was a child. I overhear conversations and an entire situation comes to me and sometimes characters appear and tell me their story. And those details show me what wants to be written. I watch. I listen. I sense what lies beneath appearances. That's how I write.

These stories are my offering. Some of them are true or based on truth and others are pure fiction. You be the judge.

Raven Wolfe, 2017

"*The pages are still blank, but there is a miraculous feeling of the words being there, written in invisible ink and clamoring to become visible.*"

—Vladimir Nabokov

"*I write entirely to find out what I am thinking,*
What I'm looking at,
What I see and what it means.
What I want and what I fear."

—Joan Didion

www.ingramcontent.com/pod-product-compliance
Lightning Source LLC
Chambersburg PA
CBHW021459250626
47154CB00004BA/1571